Enemy Me

J Carrell Jones

Mythical Legends Publishing

Enemy Me is a work of fiction. The characters, incidents, and dialogs are products of the author's imagination and are not to be construed as real. Any resemblance to actual events or persons, living or dead, is entirely coincidental.

Mythical Legends Publishing

Printed in the United States of America
9 8 7 6 5 4 3 2

Enemy Me

J Carrell Jones

Chapter 1

Pete had slipped passed the first set of guards undetected. The second set would be the problem. He lifted up the binoculars and scanned the structure in front of him. A service door off to one side. He checked his watch. It was ten past midnight and the guard shift change was about to happen in three minutes. That was his window of opportunity. Get in, get to the freight elevator, enter the code and take the thing to the labs. There he would set off the explosives. It would set the company back a few years giving the others some time. He checked his vest straps by giving then a quick yank. The pack was a bit heavy, but what did you expect from 20 kilograms of Pent?

Pete Walker woke up with a start. He wasn't supposed to be here. Not this place. Not this time. He reached up and felt the oxygen mask tightly over his mouth and nose. That was good, but he still wasn't supposed to be here. He couldn't. Damn! Another failure. And with that another chance at redemption he supposed. Maybe justice, too. All of which didn't matter at the moment. Something or someone had killed him. He took a deep breath and tested his eyes.

The filtered light had a green tint to it, so the stinging shock of using his eyes for the first time wasn't so overly painful, just maybe annoying. He took another deep breath and tested his hands. Each finger flexed. That was good. He looked up at a blinking display board over his head. It flashed "Purge in progress. Please standby." He looked around and spotted the readout displays to his right. Little monitors flashed and displayed numbers and text. One display was counting down. Another was scrolling odd bits of information, like "You can do it!", "This time for sure!", "So close, yet so far!", "It's time to leave. Prepare." That he thought odd. He looked over at the monitor that was displaying a countdown of sorts. Then he remembered. "Purge in progress." He looked up and saw two metal rings. He grabbed them. Seconds later he felt the floor underneath his feet vanish. The green tinted fluid slipped away from his eyesight. He remembered the process now. He waited until the fluid completely drained. The system would cycle through several procedures. Purge was first, wash was second. Release was third. He counted to three and the floor came back. Seconds later the container he was in filled with some clear fluid – water he thought. It was warm and turbulent, like a washing machine. Minutes ticked by as the chamber filled, circulated, and drained several times. The little countdown display kept track and reminded him he was not the original. Intellectually he understood he was not the original. Waking up in a thick green goo fluid reinforced that too. When the countdown display reached zero he was hit with a blast of hot air. It whirled around him rapidly. He was dry in seconds. He lowered himself far enough to feel the grid floor and tested his legs. Strong, firm, stable.

He let go of the overhead rings and with his weight fully supported by his feet he unsnapped his harness. There was something he was supposed to remember. The cloning process was perfect, the memory transfer not so much. There were gaps for sure, but were they important pieces missing? He looked around the cylindrical chamber trying to spot something that would trigger the memory, an important vital memory. The mask? No. It was still on his face, supplying oxygen. The readouts? No. The Grid floor? Couldn't be, but close. The chamber door? The door. That was it. He reached out and pushed. Locked. The keypad next to the door? Embarrassment hit. Of course, it was the keypad. Getting out of here was important. He let his hand drift over the pad and fingers pushed in a code he hadn't known he knew. Nevertheless, the inner door lock mechanism worked and he heard a loud audible click. The glass door whooshed up out of sight.

Pete stepped out and felt a chill. There were five empty chambers to the right of his and twelve chambers of different sizes to the left. He thought, "Five tries, five failures, five deaths." But there was still something he couldn't remember. Of course it was going to nag at him for a while. Then his stomach rumbled. He "remembered" what an empty stomach felt like. In this case, everything was going to be "remembered" and used for the very first time. He made his way to the kitchen. "Okay," he said out loud, "that was easy. But if I remember this so clearly, why do I think I'm forgetting something?" He walked through the entry way and found a sandwich waiting for him. Interesting. One of two things is going on here he thought. I made this for myself, or someone else is here. He stepped up to the table. The sandwich was cut diagonally. That was his clue to himself that it was meant for him. A glass of water and a computer tablet were next to the sandwich.

Pete sat down and starting eating. Thin slices of Turkey, Havarti cheese, Romaine lettuce, some sliced tomato, and deli horseradish sauce embedded in baguette bread. He tapped the tablet.

The screen brightened to the local news agency. In big bold letters, "Suicide bomber exploded high explosives on the 30th floor of the Taylor building. 30 died, 120 injured."

"Jesus!" Pete uttered after a bite. He committed suicide by explosive vest. Pity, but it had to have been number five. Why else would he set the tablet to show this first? But thirty died?!? Was it really necessary? He himself, of course, did not set the bomb off. He did not kill all those people. But it was him who did. Not physically. He did it. The same mind did . . . maybe. Which of course begged the question, 'was he the same person?' "I am a clone, yes, but am I number five?" He noticed the date of the article. A twenty year separation between himself and Prime. Six clones in twenty years. Short life expectancy at the very least. He finished the sandwich and followed it with the glass of water. He made his way through the passage way to the bathroom. Pete prime had some serious money to build this place. It was large and self-sustaining it seemed. He walked through the bathroom door and found the urinal. He walked up to it, looked down, and laughed. Arrogant bastard gave himself a bigger dick. Well, why not? He, and by default, himself were brilliant. Decades ahead of everyone in the field of gene therapy and cloning. Maybe next time he'd clone himself as a woman . . . a woman . . . the twelve chambers of different sizes. Several were kid size. He didn't, did he? Pete finished, washed his hands and made his way back into the chamber room. He hurried past his chamber and pried through the glass doors of the others. He did do it! The next two chambers housed females. The next three after that had one boy and two girls. They looked to be about 16. The one after that had a Pete that looked 6 feet tall. Number thirteen was a dwarf. Pretty heartless he thought, but Prime didn't know what the future held. He could walk outside and find a world full of little people. Number fourteen and fifteen was him but different. African and Asian. Interesting. Prime was mixed, but to create clones in specific races? Sixteen and seventeen were white females – one blond, one ginger. Number eighteen was at least seven feet tall and extremely bulky. Prime figured if eighteen was needed the end of days was called for. Eighteen would be the final run. The big guy would do the job by brute force. That was something to fear.

Chapter 2

Forrest Taylor looked down at chaos. Even though he was 130 stories up the many vehicles on ground level could still be seen. Little people and little trucks, cars, and ambulances at work. A suicide bomber managed to enter the building and destroy a highly guarded secret part of the building. Heads would roll figuratively, if not literally. It had been twenty years since he and Pete founded Forever Life, Inc. This was his flagship project, which was now setback a few months at best. Absolutely a pity. A new class of drugs, Transgenetics, finished the FDA trials. The level 1 and level 2 drugs were slotted for phase two of clinical rollout. Tests had been going well and on schedule for phase three. The project was not in jeopardy, but the shareholders were nervous. Fuck'em, he thought. The Vultures. Waiting to make a killing. They hadn't thought of the big picture, no. Just only the Bitcoin that would give them uber luxury. This was beyond simple gene therapy, this ultimately was immortality. This was transformation at the gene level. Every parents' wildest dream come true. Smart babies, brave babies, strong babies, ultra-beautiful babies. A Transgenetic pill for any and everything. Cancer? Gone. Colds?

Gone. Bad eyesight? Corrected. All with a set of pills. All engineered to work with the individual patient – for a price, of course. The Affordable Care Act would cover level one and two of Transgenetic, but not beyond. Levels three and above would be the money makers. Take some pills before bed, go into a coma, wake up several days later different, but the same. Baldness, obesity, impotence, weak, frail, ugly, all of the above? No more. Cured. Brilliant!

Forrest turned and sat back down at his desk. The email message waiting light blinked in the upper right corner. He clicked the OPEN message icon on a small area of his desktop.

Photos of the bomber appeared. It was Pete. The man was very insistent. How many clones had he made? Seven? How many more would he throw at him?

The room chime sounded.

Forrest said, "Enter."

Gordon Piper, his head Geneticist, walked through the door. Thank goodness the blast hadn't harmed him. Gordon was smart, not brilliant, but had enough intuitive insight to make rather startling leaps in theory, which translated into good data, results, and money. It was probably his assistant, Sandra Spaulding, who ultimately cracked the code. But Levels 3 and 4 were most likely a direct result of his unorthodox way of solving puzzles.

"Yes, Gordon?"

"Mr. Taylor, worse news yet. The entire floor destroyed. All personnel lost."

"Pity," Forrest said. "We'll have to send out condolence letters of course."

Gordon nodded.

"And the data?"

"Saved off site. The equipment has been destroyed. That'll take months to reconstruct."

Equipment gone. Forrest thought a moment. "We'll have to go off the map next time or bury the processing plants deep."

Gordon nodded. "It was Pete, wasn't it?"

Forrest nodded. "We're going to have to get serious about dealing with him."

Gordon nodded again. "Seven clones?"

"Yes."

"He'll have to modify the geno and phenotypes if he wants the clones to remain stable."

Forrest nodded. He understood what Gordon was getting at. After nine iterations the subsequent clones would probably suffer major internal organ damage. Maybe his was the last or next to last clone. He could only hope so. "How long to startup?"

"Eight months."

"That bad?"

Gordon nodded. "We'll need to hire more talent. I'm not comfortable with the Chinese. Some of them seemed to be working for other interests. Maybe the Canadians this time. I've read some rather brilliant pieces coming out of that country."

"I'll leave hiring and retooling up to you. I'll send an email to accounting and request they give you access to maintenance funds. 100 million enough?"

Gordon thought a moment. "Half a bill would be better."

Forrest blinked several times. "R&D funds then. The board green lighted two bills. If you can guarantee me a startup in three months I'll okay the full amount."

"Let me work on that. I rather be accurate in a timeframe than shooting in the dark."

He liked that about Gordon. The man wasn't much into swaging things. He'd rather be known for at least giving a problem some thought.

Forrest asked, "Tomorrow too soon?"

Gordon smiled, "About Noon. I'll take the rest of the day off and work out the details. I'll leave security to work with the locals on investigating and cleaning up the mess." He turned and walked out.

Forrest watched the man as he disappeared behind the closing door. Cold and calloused. The nature of big business making billions. He was still in his glass house, so he refrained from casting stones, at least very large ones.

Chapter 3

Pete found his way to the main computer room. So far he "remembered" things both necessary and mundane. As he stepped through the doorway the lights came on.

"Good morning, Doctor Walker. How are you?" A Verdi baritone voice seemed to come from everywhere.

Pete nearly jumped. That he hadn't remembered, not quite like that. A voice from a computer terminal perhaps. Maybe on his Tablet. "Morning?"

"I read the news. You have my deepest condolences. I am . . ."

"A computer?"

There was a pause. "Yes, Doctor Walker. I run the facility. Pete Prime installed me on day one."

Pete sat in the main chair. "I see." There were a total of five computer terminals. Pete occupied the middle one. "So, why do I not remember you if you were installed twenty years ago?"

"Doctor, I cannot answer that." The computer's voice was smooth.

"Cannot or will not?"

"Let me rephrase my answer, please. I do not know the answer to your question. Number five and two did not remember, but one and three did. You'll find further gaps in your memory no doubt. As you know the cloning process is perfect. The memory transference and its means are not."

Pete weighted that answer against truth and total bullshit. "Fair enough. Did number five leave anything for me?"

The computer said, "Yes he did. Several items in fact."

Pete thought the exchange creepy. The computer seemed too good with speech. "You are a real person, aren't you?"

The silence settled in between the two for a minute.

"Well? You are real, aren't you? I mean as in AI real?"

The center display screen came to life. His face appeared with a relaxed smile. "Mike," number five said over his shoulder, "I'm ready."

"Yes, George. Recording now."

Number five cleared his voice. "Number six, sorry I couldn't welcome you into the world personally. I should have started recording a daily log day one, but . . ." He shrugged. "You'll discover things tend to get lost in translating and we Walkers tend to become self-absorbed." Five's smile was alarming. It was a bit unnerving to be on the receiving end. "Remember that, okay. First, change your first name."

Odd Pete thought.

Number five continued, ". . . I am not Pete. Neither are you. We are our own individuals." The image leaned forward. "Yes we share memories with Pete, but we are not him. The moment you opened your eyes you became your own person." He leaned back.

"Remember me as George. Keep the family name but lose the first. Seriously. It took me several months to understand that. Kevin, number four, told me to change my name. I fought it. Just fought it. Then one day I realized Pete and I had nothing substantive in common. I read romance, he read non-fiction. I like Pistachio ice cream. He was a vanilla man. You getting the picture yet?"

On the surface he felt he understood. "I am unique," he thought. Well, of course. The Pete twenty years ago would have been him, but not now. He was dead . . . assuming the reason he lived was because he was dead as well as numbers one through five.

"About Mike. Don't ask if he is a real person. Mike will give you the silent treatment for days. If you did ask apologize, now. Seriously. Apologize. You'll need his help."

Pete said, "Mike, I am sorry. I won't question you again about being real."

Mike said, "Forgiven. There is more."

Pete smiled. Interesting.

"Number six, I'd like to tell you to forget our quest. You know, live your own life. Start a family. Have two and one-half kids running around. . ." George suddenly looked ten years older. "Forrest Taylor has to be stopped. Brother six, Forrest has to be stopped." He leaned back and looked sad. "I've been fighting this bastard for six years now. I've been able to uncover a lot as were the others. Kevin, Pete 3, Pete 2, and Eugene. Forrest's plan is worse than anyone can imagine. Sick bastard." Suddenly George stood up and walked away. "Mike, pause recording please. Thanks." The image of a receding George froze in mid step.

Pete waited for a minute, then asked, "Mike, something wrong with the video?"

"No. I was waiting for you to ask."

Pete paused in a thought, "Waiting for me to . . ."

The video resumed. George sat back down. "Okay, good, I do have your attention. Look, the cloning process is perfect. Too perfect. Do you remember this?" George held up a picture of a woman. She was a redhead, light smile, white skin, clean teeth perfectly aligned. He lowered the picture and leaned in close to the screen. "I didn't. I still don't. Mike had to fill me in with missing gaps in my memory. I'm not sure if the missing gaps is from the transference process or intentional intervention. All of us have this memory lapse. Mine is with Stephanie." He lifted the picture up to the camera and pulled it away. "Number seven is going to remember less than you do. Number eight less more than seven, and so on and so on. Number eighteen will remember nothing. He'll have one thought. Destroy. If he wakes up, then Forrest succeeded and all of humankind, at least in nations where the wealthy can afford the drugs, he'll have one preprogrammed thought. Soon after he wakes he'll double in size. He'll get no last message because he won't understand. Mike will send him immediately to the surface. No help, no prep, nothing. Because it won't matter. He'll destroy. He'll run the distance from here to the Taylor Building and destroy. Everything. Everything. He's not number eighteen, he's Omega." George looked up at some part of the room. "Everything." He rubbed his chin. "Enough of doomageddon." He smiled. "I left you an envelope, among other things, with a list of do's and don'ts for your new life. You, my friend, are twenty years out of step. Remember that. It is no longer the 20th dark ages. Space travel to the Moon is normal, but not by the United States. Gay marriage is the norm. So are GEMPs. Genetically Engineered Chimps. The US Government gave them full citizenship ten years ago. We've elected a black President and a woman President. Twice. The Middle-East is fucked since we no longer depend on their oil, of which they have none. We export 23% of the world's oil needs and Iran had been nuked, by Israel. North Korea fell, Russia bankrupt . . . again, and China had a severe housing collapse, went through a depression and lost a war. You have allies on the outside. Becky will freak . . . oh, yes. We do love." George gave his patented alarming smile again. "You also have enemies. We'll always have enemies. I gave you a list of 'em. There's plenty. Homeland Security is at the local level. Surveillance cameras cover 90 percent of the city. Androids are reality and marijuana, prostitution, and assisted suicide are legal. What's that gotta say about the country?" George paused in thought. "Two more things. Trust Mike. He's been watching and protecting us for a number of years — twenty for you, fifteen for me. He knows everything. He's our Mentor. The second thing is . . ." George got teary eyed. He bit his lower lip. "I left you a memory card. Technology has made the transference better and easier but not perfect. You'll get most of what I lived through the last five years. I regret not having started a family, but knowing that Pete left a vast assortment of clones the Walkers may indeed live on through normal means . . . one day. Hopefully, my sacrifice did some damage. If not maybe you can do something better. Think out of the box is all I can say. Good luck, brother.

Good luck." A smiling George faded to black.

21

Chapter 4

Pete stared at the monitor for a long while. Twenty years. That long. Pete thought, "Change my name to what?" He heard a deep cough, but ignored it.

Mike said, "May I be of assistance?"

Pete remained deep in thought.

Mike coughed louder breaking Pete's thoughts.

Pete looked up and around. "Yes?"

Mike repeated, "May I be of assistance?"

"To what?"

"Your name dilemma."

"Who said I was thinking about my name?"

Silence.

It stretched out to a full minute.

Pete broke the silence first. Damn computer he thought. Mind reader? "Thanks for the offer."

Mike said, "No, I am not."

"What?"

"I am not a mind reader."

"How in the world did you know what I was thinking?"

Silence.

Exasperation crept into Pete's voice. "Well?!?"

"You may not be Pete prime, but you think like him.

I've had twenty years of experience."

Pete said, "Point taken."

Silence.

"Mike, thank you. I want to think this through a few moments."

"While you're thinking through your name dilemma I'd like to give you the rest of George's items."

"Okay?"

"Do not be startled . . ."

"About what?"

He heard Mike's voice directly behind him "This, sir."

Pete, startled, turned to see an Android. "Jesus Christ!"

The Android said, "My intention was not to startle you."

"Intention failed." But Pete was intrigued. He got up and walked around the machine. Amazing he thought. "What can it do?"

The Android stood six feet tall. Most of its body was made of tubes and wiring. Small composite plates of different shapes were placed around his limbs and chest. They gave the illusion he had calves, biceps, shoulders, and pecs. There were even two plates shaped and placed so it looked like he had buttocks.

The Android answered, "It? It, sir, can do a lot." And it held out a very large envelope.

Pete grabbed it.

The Android held onto the envelope a few seconds longer than it should have.

Pete watched as it turned and walked away. "Does it have a name?"

"You could ask the next time you see him." Mike replied.

"I suppose I could. What other surprises are in store for me?"

"There is someone sleeping in your bed."

Dumbstruck, Pete dropped the envelope. "What?!? A Guest?!?" He walked to "his" room and stopped. The door was ajar. He pushed it open slowly and stepped into the dimly lit room. A form was curled up underneath the blankets. He stepped in and the floor creaked.

The form moved, then a head lifted up. The covers slipped away to show a dirty blonde woman yawning. She looked around and spotted Pete. "Hey, babe!" She said. "You back so soon. Everything went okay?"

Stunned, Pete lost his voice. He coughed and held up a hand. He motioned for her to lay back down while backing out.

She did, yawned again, and said, "Okay, babe. See you in a few hours."

Pete closed the door and made it back to the command room. "What the . . . ?"

Mike said, "Her name is Rebecca. George calls her Becky. She is his . . ."

"What?!?" Pete interrupted.

"She is also one of those allies George mentioned."

"But . . . but . . . she . . ."

"Is unaware that George is no longer here, which by the way, you are the last to awake upon the death of a previous clone."

"Oh, this is just getting better and better." He placed his palm against his forehead and slowly shook his head.

"The envelope."

"The what? Oh, that." Pete reached down and

grabbed it. He walked over to the center seat, moved the keyboard out of the way and emptied its contents onto desk. Photos, a wallet, gun, knife, camera, cell phone, a bottle of pills, a passport, car keys, reading glasses, a folded piece of paper, and small black box with a wind up key in the back. He stared at the content for a few seconds. "Okay, Mike, I'm not getting this. I need help."

"George started making recordings weeks after he awoke. Number Four, Kevin, gave him a similar recording as George gave you. Kevin left George everything except the reading glasses, bottle of pills, and the small black box. Over time, of course, the contents have increased.

The center monitor lit up with George sitting at the desk. His hair was messy and he had a five-day old beard. His eyes were bloodshot with hooded eyelids. "This is madness. It's been two weeks and I haven't slept well. Kevin, that's the name number four chose, said that Forrest's company Forever Life submitted an investigational New Drug application to CDER. Apparently, he was going to sabotage the application, but didn't succeed. I woke up two weeks ago and binged on all the information about Forrest and Forever Life, Inc. This is crazy. Forrest is our Alpha! He was the first successful clone and we are working against him!" The screen went black.

Pete sat there for a few moments thinking. Number four, presumably, discovered/revealed Forrest as Prime's first successful clone. Incredible!

A new image appeared. "Forrest is out of his mind. He has to be. I see why, Pete Prime broke ties with him and made this place. Transgenetics can transform the entire world to something good. Think about it. A pill that acts as a transport and vector for radical morphologic change, but Forrest has a secret agenda. He wants to make the world shaped in his image." The screen went black a few seconds, then George reappeared. "I've been alive for about six months now. This world is amazing! Cars that drive themselves? Androids? Of which I'm going to have to make one. Space travel? Vacations in Earth's orbit. Opportunities? Endless." The screen went black.

Pete heard from behind him, "Hey Babe. You hadn't looked at those old vids for months. What's up?"

He slowly turned and saw Becky standing in the doorway. She was dressed in a translucent blue teddy. She had fuzzy rabbit faced slippers on and she had bed head. Pete thought "My 'ucking God! George was one lucky son-of-a-bitch."

She walked up to him and leaned down.

Pete regretted he flinched. He bit his lip, but said nothing.

Becky frowned, stood up and carefully gave Pete a once over. She stared into his eyes, then walked out the room.

Pete followed her. Dread set in when he realized she was headed to the Cloning chamber. As he entered the room he spotted her on her knees crying. He stopped just out of arms reach. "I'm sorry," was all he could say.

She turned on him. Her eyes red and puffy. "Why!" She screamed at him. "Why are you doing this?!? Why!"

Pete backed up, his shoulders drooped. He looked down.

Becky screamed, "This is not fair!"

He could do nothing but watch. Suddenly she jumped up and ran over to the door. A heavy axe was attached to the adjacent wall. She pulled it from its cradle and dragged the heavy thing passed all the chambers to stop at number 18.

Pete realized what she was about to do. He yelled, "Stop! Not yet!"

She gave him a death stare and said, "This is total bullshit! All of it is bullshit! Let's just let him take the whole fuckin' place down and end this madness!"

He raced to her side just as she lifted the heavy axe over her shoulder. He grabbed the handle on the down swing, stopping her from smashing the glass.

She yelled, "Let it go, clone!"

Pete's head snapped back. 'Let it go, clone!' she said. Clone. As in copy, duplicate, not the original. He lost his temper. "Get a hold of yourself you fucking idiot! This is not about you! It's about the world." He tossed the axe across the room. Anger gripped firmly now, "You. Need. To. Fucking. Grow. Up!" He stared into her eyes and did not blink.

She tried to stare him down, but Pete was too far into his anger to care. Silly bitch he thought.

"You think I asked to be here?!?"

Her eyes dropped.

"I'm more than a victim here. I'm twenty years out of date and everyone I knew is either dead, old, or I can't remember them. I have problems bigger than yours. I am truly sorry George is gone. There are so many questions I need to ask, but all I have is a sensitive computer and you! And from where I'm standing I'm pretty much fucked!"

Becky's eyes teared up. Seconds later she ran out

the room and disappeared down the hallway.

Pete sighed heavily. He let his anger cool before he spoke. "Mike?" He said but he got no response. "Sorry if I offended you."

Mike remained silent.

Pete walked over to the axe, grabbed it, and placed it back into its cradle. He walked out the room, sad. All this in less than an hour of his new life. Maybe he should have let her smash the glass. Maybe not.

Chapter 5

Pete sat back down in front of the computer screen. He waited several seconds. Nothing. "Mike, I apologized. I am sorry."

Nothing.

Pete counted to ten. "Mike, please, continue with the videos."

Nothing.

Pete yelled, "Goddamnit! What do you expect of me? I don't know you and I'm trying to cope here! Give me some answers!"

Nothing.

"Fine then. Can you at least give me access to the Internet? The Internet is still around, right?"

The screen lit up and displayed some icons. Pete clicked on a world icon. The application ran and displayed a blank screen. An empty address bar had a blinking cursor waiting for data. Pete typed in "Search engine."

Google appeared. He let out a sigh and said more to himself than to Mike, "Finally! Something I remember." He typed in "Pete Walker". 37,600,000 results in .002 seconds. He added cloning. A Wikipedia entry was at the top of the list. Several pictures of him appeared underneath that. One picture was his face, the rest of what he looked like at 10 years his senior. So, I'll start to grey in ten years? Then he remembered George only lived for six. A rather dumb and expensive way to achieve youthful immortality. He clicked on the Wikipedia entry. He, meaning Pete, first died fifteen years ago. That meant the average clone life expectancy sucked. He sat back and stared at the contents again. The wallet. Let's start with the wallet. It was brown leather with worn edges, standard two-fold with the expected number of credit card slots, all of which were filled with various cards. A platinum AMEX in George's name. Nice! A Visa, MasterCard, Discover card. Some food card of sorts. He would have to ask Mike about it later. That is, if the computer started talking to him again. Maybe Becky would be a better source of information now. Maybe. A driver's license with George's face and name on it and a piece of paper, folded.

Pete unfolded the piece of paper:

Tonight. Alone.
Waterfront dock 2
100K

Cloak and dagger. Quaint.

The screen lit up and George's face appeared. He said, "Thanks, Mike. I'm getting the hang of this. Hey number six and others, hopefully not others, but anyway, I left you puzzle pieces. Some of the items were left for me. I've added a few new ones. So, now that I have your attention I'll go through each one. The photos. Very important. Number six, you are really number seven . . ."

Pete held his breath.

"George continued, ". . . you know what I'm talkin' 'bout. I'll assume that others, at some point, will be viewing this in the future. So, forgive me brother six for stating the obvious between us. . ."

Pete absently nodded.

" . . . Twenty years ago, cloning required the isolation of certain cells – stem cells. Those were the cells used in the process. They could've been any cell in the body but they had to meet certain criteria. For me, it took three months, from the records it took four months for you. Number 18 took nine. Once the right cells are found, they're cultured. These are the base cells used to make all of us and they do have limits. For one is the shortened telomeres, of which Pete's process negates the negative results. But because of the process, seven identical clones can successfully be created. After that we have to modify the geno- and phenotypes. Maybe it's nature's way of keeping human vanity at bay. That's why Pete cloned us, after you, as females, kids, and different races. They are us, but also someone else. In a sense, they really are our brothers and sisters. I say all this to stress that, brother six, you are the last of the Pete originals. In mind? That went with Pete three."

Pete said, "Mike, please pause the video."

George's image stopped in mid speech.

"Will you talk to me now? Please?"

The silence went on for three minutes before Mike said, "I will talk to you, now."

"First, what did I do or say to you to make you mad at me?"

A full minute ticked by. "You made her cry."

"I see." He did actually. "You like Becky." Pete said it as a statement, not a question.

Five minutes went by. "I do."

Pete nodded. "Understood. I will try not to hurt her feelings again, but because I've only known the both of you for less than two hours, please forgive me for any faux pas I may commit going forward. I am a stranger here."

Mike answered almost immediately, "Understood, sir."

"May I ask you another question?"

"Certainly."

"It's about Pete Prime."

"Please ask. I am here to help."

"Can you see a difference in me and Pete Prime?"

Silence for about three minutes.

Pete wondered if the silence was the equivalent of a computer sigh or Mike running hundreds, if not, thousands of simulations?

"Yes, sir. There is."

Pete held his breath.

"You have more patience. Pete Prime was rather impatient. Physical appearance, speech, and gait are identical to a Pete Walker at 39 years old. There hasn't been enough time to discern other differences. Please ask me again in 24 hours."

Pete nodded. "Thank you, Mike."

"You are welcome, sir. Should I resume the video?"

Pete smiled. "Yes, please. Thank you." This one he decided worked best with pleasantries. 'Incredible', he thought. Totally incredible. Eerily, Mike sounded and acted human. Was it that Mike 'evolved'? Or was he installed with a conscious? Pete decided once Mike got to know him he would ask.

" . . . For some reason, the memory transference changes slightly with each use. That's why I didn't remember Stephanie. Mike has mentioned that with each clone we seem to be more reflective, more thoughtful. We are not as reactionary as Pete Prime. If you have time, work on it or not." He smiled. "You can always leave it to our brothers and sisters to ponder over, that is if you . . ." he coughed. ". . . decide to wake them." He leaned in close to the screen. "Interesting that you have that option." His right eye brow raised up. "I wondered why Pete Prime did that. Are we that much a super genius as to play chess twenty years in the future? By the way, you may have met or not met Becky." His smile was slight but noticeable. A few seconds later, "More on that later." He leaned back. "The wallet, I'm sure you've already rifled through it. Nothing special there except that it is 20 years old. Mike can help you get a legal license with proper papers to back everything up. The same for credit cards. Mike, hopefully, started inserting purchase history into the national databases. We have a drop box at the local post office. It's within walking distance, which is good, because it'll help you to learn the streets. Slow is well, fast is hell."

Pete nodded.

"Now the photos. The Red head is Pete Alpha. Pete Prime and Alpha started Forever Life, Inc. together. The records show them as twin brothers – one of which was separated at birth only later to be reunited with family. Good story. Reads like a good mystery." That smile again. "As you can see, Pete Alpha, now named Forrest, looks nothing like us . . ." He leaned in close. ".

. . that's the power of Transgenetics. It really is amazing and powerful, but it is a time bomb. Prolong usage ultimately changes the phenotype. Very subtle over a period of years, but eventually, the user starts to look like Forrest. Prolonged use also causes sterility. In most cases, the host will be beyond reproductive age anyway, but here is the kicker. At some point, all users will have nearly the same DNA sequence. As in brother, sister, mother, father." He paused and let that settle in. "At some point in the future humans will be inbreeding. Oh, we may figure it out before it is too late, but why take that chance? Through different means Mike, I, and our brothers have tried to sound the alarm through academic papers, protest, and other means. But a billion dollars can go a long way in suppressing the truth." He shrugged. "The other photos are of staff and his top scientist, Gordon. I'm hoping to eliminate most, if not all. Gordon is the one who really must go. He's the one who put all the pieces together. His assistant Sandra Spaulding broke the code, but he figured out the proper sequence for Transgenetics to work. Prep the recipient, introduce modifiers embedded in a pill. The adenoviruses are enclosed in small casings that survive the digestive tract long enough to enter the blood stream. From there they find host cells, and turn on or off trigger hormones and proteins needed to work the magic. Brother, they change the very nature on how the host cell works and functions. Brilliant, but not without a cost. This is a payment we should never make. Incidentally, I really did mean to come back, but death seems to be irrelevant when you have brothers and sisters who can at any time tap into my last thoughts. We all started getting very philosophical about life. It would be nice to think that I died of old age and forgot to update this recording, in which case Forrest was stopped and the world went about its busy life. Existentialism is pretty heavy stuff. We are all individuals who just happens to spring from the same well. Our very existences precedes essence, brother. From here forward you are who you are. Seriously, you'll have to stop thinking of yourself as Pete. Forrest did. Kevin did, I did. Our brothers and sisters will certainly think so. It's your turn, which brings me to that small black box." George lowered his head. "Of course, if you are looking at this I never did make it back." He took a deep breath, "The box is for Becky, which, hopefully, you two have met already and hopefully things have not gotten too weird. Read what I wrote and please give her the box. I'll trust you to know when and where." He cleared his throat after several moments of silence. "The bottle of pills are from pre-trails. Kevin was able to get a hold of them. I left you enough to study. The gun is special. 3D printed and holds ten shots. Eight now. It is completely detection proof. The passport is mine, of course, Mike will get you a new one. It'll take a few months. The glasses you'll need later. Trust me." He winked. "Once you get your license you'll need to get around. Becky can help with that. Our car is the latest model and essentially needs no driver. You'll find out later. Google made good on their threat on making driverless cars a reality, and the world is a safer place for it. The knife, well, that is the same as the gun. I've used it twice – don't ask." He smiled. "I said Google made the world a safer place, not the neighborhoods. That's something different. What? All those years learning martial arts and you thought you'd never need it? The future is great but it is far from utopia. Not quite dystopia but damn close. Despite one political power trying very hard not letting the other political party drive us into the ground we still got there. The economic divide is bigger than ever. Becky can best instruct in that. And the cell phone. It's to Forrest. I'm going to leave it at that. Talk to Becky about it, but remember this, 'Enemies of my friends may not be my enemies.' The camera has my latest shots of the Forrest Building. Probably useless now, but . . ." He shrugged. "There are other Easter Egg videos I left. Some relevant, some not, some total bullshit. Six years is a long time for us, Brother. Live yours and then some. After Pete Prime passed, Pete Two went into total isolation. He left one day to confront Forrest. That was After Pete four years. Never came back. The news feed says he was struck by a car. Killed instantly. Pete three lived longer – died seven AP. He studied Forrest. Even challenged him. He met a horrible and lonely death. Kevin lived longer to 15 AP. If you are getting this last addendum to this video you're at 21 AP. There is one last thing." George seemed to be considering his words. "There is a memory all of us cannot remember. It's a pin-point of thought that just nags at us. Mike can't or won't explain it. The data records only show that something was there. Pete Prime removed a piece of his memory from the process. Maybe you'll be the one to uncover it." The screen went blank.

Pete sighed. "Mike?"

"Yes, sir."

"What do you think?"

Silence.

Pete stared at the screen for about two minutes.

Kevin appeared. Pete could tell it was him but not him and not George. They really did seem to be different. "Number three was captured. The drugs, unofficially, made human trials that day. Transgenetics was able to breeze through initial FDA testing because Forever Life, Inc. had the perfect subject, Pete three. From what I can uncover they kept him alive for a year. I remember being woken up four times only to be placed back in hiber at least four times. Mike tells me he could not control the process. He had to let the safe guards take control when the system received some life telemetry from Number three. He died four times and they brought him back for more testing. Bastards!" The screen went blank.

"I see," Pete said. He sat staring at a blank screen for a while.

Mike finally said, "Pete. It is time for dinner."

Pete reached over to the black box. He opened it and took out the note. Tears streamed down his cheek as he read the note. Several drops hit the paper and slightly stained some of the letters. He folded it back up and placed it back in the box. After he wound the small turnkey at the back he got up and made his way to the kitchen.

Chapter 6

Pete walked into the kitchen area. The table had been set for two. A vase and some Amethyst were placed in the center. Becky sat at one end.

She said, "I was hoping you'd make it here before I started eating."

Pete noticed she did not begin with 'Hey babe'. He sat down still holding the small black box. The box George meant to give her. His special gift of love. He had planned to return, maybe. So many branches of 'what if's'. Mostly all bullshit and wishful thinking, but a few had legs --- if given the chance to run. He sat down and placed the box on the table next to a glass of water.

Becky eyed the box but didn't say a thing. She said, "Mike, ready."

The android walked up to the table holding a bowl of salad in each hand. He placed one in front of Becky and the other in front of Pete, turned and walked away.

Becky said, "His name is Prax." She pronounced it 'Praks'.

Pete said "Prax . . ."

The android paused on its way toward the kitchen cooking area.

Pete continued, ". . . as in praxis? Action?"

She nodded. "Most appropriate one would think." She raised her left brow and gave him a light smile.

Prax resumed walking into the kitchen.

Pete blushed and smiled back. He looked around wondering what to say next. He thought, 'you are a social clod.'

Becky's smile broadened and she lifted the salad fork.

Pete grabbed the dinner fork. He always thought one needed a fork with the longest teeth to get as much leaf as possible.

Becky stifled a laugh.

Pete looked up, "What?"

Becky smiled, "Nothing. Use whatever you like to eat salad. It's not like the arrangement is some form of artistic post neo-functionalism."

Pete stabbed some romaine and red cabbage cuts. The dressing was perfect. Not thick enough to mask the taste but thin enough to not be tasted. "This is delicious. Thank you."

Becky finished chewing, said, "Don't thank me. Prax and Mike have been cooking for us for years."

Pete forced his smile. '. . . been cooking for years' she said, '. . . been cooking for us.' "Becky, I'm sorry I lost my temper . . ."

"Already forgotten. Moving forward, okay?"

Pete paused for a moment. Just like that? Forgotten?

She nodded, "Yes, just like that." She stabbed salad, scooped it into her mouth, and started chewing. She never took her eyes off him.

Pete swallowed hard and grabbed the glass of water and drank deeply. He patted his lips and pretended to be amused by tablecloth lint.

Becky smiled. "I'm not a mind reader, but I do have the advantage." She thought he was just like George the first day they met. Then her smile vanished. Damn you George, you left me. Will all this be worth it in the end? She sighed. "What's in the black box?"

Pete stared into her eyes. Pressure gripped his heart. Vise squeezing pressure crushed hard. Tears welled up. He grabbed the box, got up from the table and walked it over to her. He laid the box carefully next to the glass of water. He sat back down and finished his salad, quietly.

Becky placed the fork down and eyed the box. She lifted the lid and pulled out the note first. The little fairy stood up and twirled slowly as the song "Sweet Dreams" tinked on.

My dearest Becky,

In all my lives I don't think I have ever been happiest. You kept me going. You supported me emotionally, mentally, spiritually. On the days I doubted my own existence you applied logic and passion. I am forever grateful for your love and I truly am sorry that I am gone . . . temporarily. If number six is giving you this then everything went terribly wrong. I did mean to return, but . . . and we talked about this often . . . the waiter brought me my check. Luckily, you fell in love with a man with cat lives. I'll wake up in the morning and forget who I am, but will have you to remind me what it is worth fighting for. Please

*forgive me and don't be mad at me, or me.
I am just a stranger in a strange land now
and I need a guiding hand, a calm heart, and
a cool head to help get through and beyond
this.*

*Eternal love,
George*

Becky cried. Tears of pain, anger, sorrow, and love. She took the napkin and dabbed at her wet eyes. Then she noticed some of the letters were blurred from recent tears. She looked up. "You read this?"

Pete sat staring at a woman he hadn't known long enough to love but knew he could. It was all that easy, yet all that hard. *I am a man who has forgotten* he thought. *Will I remember? Will I want to remember?* "Sorry, but George asked me too. Something wrong?"

Becky finished wiping her eyes dry. She took a sip of water and said, "Prax?"

The Android stepped up to the table, "Yes, ma'am?"

"Wine, please. Red. Your choice."

Prax said, "Yes, ma'am. A good Spica seems to be in order." He turned and walked away.

Becky reached into the box and pulled out a small medallion. It was the one George promised her years ago. He found it. A Beatles Cavern Club medal. Practically priceless now. She placed it back in the box and sighed. A few seconds later she heard a familiar "pop".

Prax emerged from the kitchen holding a bottle marked with the label 'Fat Bastard'. He poured a healthy dose into both glasses and left.

Becky held up the glass and said, "To life."

Pete hastily picked his up, nearly spilling it, and said, "To life."

Both drank. Becky's was more so to feel numb. Pete to not feel awkward.

"So," Becky began, "have you thought about a name, yet?"

"Name?"

She nodded. "Pete, you are not, and it has been taken."

"But I am . . ." He paused. Pete? No, I am not Pete. "George said it took him months to pick a name."

She nodded. "I . . . met . . . him a few months after that."

"So, why am I more accepting of changing my name?"

"Very good question. Could be you are so far removed from the Pete. George said number one took a different name, but two and three didn't. You know about Pete Alpha?"

Pete nodded. "Forrest. Our nemesis it seems."

"Kevin understood."

"And so did George?"

She nodded.

Prax removed the now empty bowls. A minute later he came back with a tray of sizzling thin cut short ribs nested on a bed of sautéed thin sliced onions, mushrooms, bell and chili peppers. He shoveled half the amount on Pete's plate and the rest on to Becky's. He placed a small heap of white rice next to the meat and left chop sticks.

Pete stared down at his plate.

Becky moved some hair behind an ear. "You do

remember how to use chopsticks?"

He smiled, "Yeah, I do."

"Then why the hesitation? It is dead."

"This is my second meal of my new life." He looked up and caught Becky staring back.

She smiled briefly, looked down, and picked up a piece of meat with her chopsticks. She tore off a piece of meat from the bone with her teeth and chewed slowly. The meat was tender and seemed to melt into a delicious taste of savory and sweet sauce. A bit of chili pepper emerged but didn't distract as much as add to the flavor.

Pete tasted the meat and an explosion of salt, sugar, vinegar, a dozen spices, and hotness swirled across his tongue. His eyes watered as he slowly chewed the soft meat. "Whoa," he whispered.

Becky said, "I envy you, person who is not George but will soon change his name to something nice I could like."

Pete laughed. He liked Becky. "How so?"

"You've come into the world as an adult."

"I missed being a kid."

Becky paused in mid bite. She scowled. "You do?"

"Why does that surprise you?"

"Person who is not George but will soon change his name to something nice I could like, George said he hated his childhood."

"Interesting."

Becky nodded, "How can two people of the same have different views on childhood?"

Pete thought about that. He finished half the rice and a third of his main meal. "My childhood . . . that's not right . . . the childhood I remember was tough. But as a kid I had very little responsibility . . ."

Becky nodded.

". . . yeah, I had to learn, and my parents pushed an overachieving kid to continue stretching the envelope, I could just be." He bit into a chili pepper and quickly followed it with some onions and bell pepper. The wine helped, but barely. He took his napkin and dabbed at the sweat forming on his forehead.

Becky thought it cute that person who is not George but will soon change his name to something nice she could like wiped his forehead. She really did envy him. But she also pitied him. He woke to a world distressed and in need of healing. He wasn't the doctor, but maybe one of the meds prescribed. If only she could leave and start over. Like maybe one of the new colonies starting up. She finished her plate and placed the chopsticks down.

Prax stood ready. He focused on the clone and waited for him to finish eating. When the clone seemed to have had enough of the main meal he collected the dishes. Mike gave him instructions via a wireless link. One in particular was simple: Observe. This one was like the others physically, but different in several ways. Its movements were more graceful. It didn't move in fits and starts like the Original and clone 2 and 3. This one was more like the Alpha.

Becky nodded when she noticed the person who is not George but will soon change his name to something nice she could like placed his chopsticks down. The rice gone, the meat and veggies consumed. His wine glass drain, his water glass drained.

Prax took his cue from Mike and cleared the table. He placed the dishes in the sink and walked over to a very large refrigerator. Desert had already been prepared: Cucumber and Lemon-Lime sorbet with a sprinkle of sea salt. Dollops of pureed mint and sugar were placed on the side.

Becky watched as the person who is not George but will soon change his name to something nice slowly dropped his jaw. He closed his mouth and swallowed audibly.

Prax backed away and watched the clone closely. He monitored heart rate, blood pressure, and body temperature. The clone picked up the spoon and scraped a small amount of sorbet into it. It lifted the spoon to its mouth. Tears pooled at the bottom of its eyes. It took a larger amount of sorbet and placed it in its mouth. The clone's body visibly relaxed. Its body temperature dropped to 97.1, heart rate to 72, respiration 10, blood pressure 110/70. From the expression on the clone's face Prax reasoned it was content.

Chapter 7

"Kent."

Becky said, "Pardon?"

After dinner the two had moved to the "living room". It was a large area with a circular fireplace set in the center. A fire was burning and the wire mesh cage encompassing the pit kept most of the occasional burning embers from jumping too far from the fire. The two sat on a semi-circular couch near the fireplace. Pete felt comfortable enough to allow Becky to rest in his arms.

Mike was half way through playing Beethoven's Moonlight Sonata, piano No. 14.

The two had lazily reclined on the couch gazing into the fire.

"Kent. That's my new name."

Becky mused over that. Kent. Kent. Kent. Maybe. Kent reminded her of a certain mild-mannered reporter. Kent. It was easy off the tongue. Kent. She smiled. Kent. She did like it. It meant he was more than the eye could see. Kent. "Okay, Kent. Nice to meet you. My name is Elizabeth, but my inner circle calls me Becky. I'd like you to be part of that circle."

Pete who is now Kent blushed. "I'd like to be part of

that inner circle." He took a deep breath, "Hi Becky. My name is Kent. Nice to know you. I used to be a clone. Now I am my own person."

"Hello own person Kent."

The silence lingered as Piano No. 14 played on in the background at a presto agitato. Many fast arpeggios and strongly accented notes echoed off the walls. The two stared into each other's eyes.

"I am not George."

She nodded.

"You okay with that?"

She nodded again and moved closer. She nestled herself against his chest and didn't care who he was. She could dream, that was the important part.

Kent was at first startled that Becky moved closer. He hadn't expected her to get so close into his personal space, but then again, he looked and sounded like George. Probably acted like him too. It surprised him even more when she kissed him and he returned it without complaint.

Prax turned and left the room.

Mike decreased the airflow to the fireplace, letting the fire die down. He turned the vents on and dropped the room's temperature by two degrees. He hoped they would get the hint. The bedroom was one of the few places he did not have cameras installed.

Chapter 8

Kent woke with a start. He was in his bed, which felt odd but natural at the same time. His body had twenty years of upright suspended sleep embedded, but being in a prone position just seemed right on the physical level. For a moment he wondered if the entire day had been a dream. The chamber, the computer, android, the videos of someone that looked like him, the beautiful woman . . . he turned his head to the left. She was there. Sleeping on the pillow. Snoring softly. It wasn't a dream. A flood of images overwhelmed him. He. Was. A. Clone . . . which was remarkable. Conceived, cultivated, nurtured to birth age and accelerated to a specific age, and held in stasis until another cloned unit expired. But he was different. He was the last cloned unit of the original. He, also, had choices the others didn't. He could wake the others left behind. The others, in any order he presumed. He had that option, which made him unique. He was different. That was important. He had to hold onto that thought. 'Carbon-copies have the distinction of being flawed copies of the original.' He was different. Different. A word that means what? Distinct, separate, not the same as another or each other. Dissimilar. Hold onto that . . . Kent. Your name is Kent. You are Kent. "I am Kent," he said softly. Kent. Yes. He got up and walked into the bathroom. The lights came on automatically. He stood in front of the mirror and stared. "Kent," he said. Sampling the name and finally deciding it tasted well. A nice heady feel weighed by reason that lacked superficial and superfluous emotion. This was clinical. He was Kent.

Becky leisurely woke up. She yawned, stretched, and yawned again. Last night had been good. She didn't think it was great – George had turned into a great lover over the years. Kent was as George was on their first night. Cutely shy, handsomely awkward, and innocently consistent. She only had two orgasms and that was because she took control and became top. But, she was content. George was gone, but not gone. It was like he lost his memory and had to relearn things again. She was okay with that. She was also okay if he never truly loved her. Kent was not George. She was just happy to be able to be in his presence. He was his own person and she would try hard not to remind him that he was not the original but, in fact, an original himself. "Morning," she said when she saw Kent walk out of the bathroom.

Kent smiled, "Morning." They made love last night. It was great for him, but he had the feeling that she hadn't been completely satisfied. George had six years of practice, he was only, technically, one days old, which was a stupefying concept to wrap one's brain around. Literally, yesterday was nothing but firsts for him. Today would be no different, except the firsts wouldn't be as often, and seconds are never as OMG worthy as the first time.

"Any special plans today?" Becky asked.

Kent slowly shook his head while exhaling from a deep breath. "Take a walk outside? Maybe."

Becky smiled, "Probably not so close to the building. We're about a hundred feet below one of the roughest neighborhoods in the city."

"Roughest? The Everglades? It was a very prestige place . . ."

She interrupted, "Twenty plus years ago."

He got teary-eyed. "TV? TV is still around?"

She laughed, "Almost nothing but TV!" She led Kent through a hallway, he didn't remember, to a small theater of sorts. Twelve large upholstered chairs lined up in three rows with a comfortable wide center space separating two chairs on either side of it. Becky slightly titled her head to the ceiling, "Mike, anything special at this hour?"

"Yes, ma'am. The Lord Patricia of Glencoe is conducting the 23rd Highlands Title gathering at Loch Linnhe. The event highlights one million plots sold to date. It is heralded as a beacon of Conservation done right and profitably."

"Wait . . ." Kent started, "Lord Patricia? Shouldn't that be Lady Patricia?"

"Lord is now a recognized title for a female, sir. Interestingly, there are three times more female Lords than there are male Ladies."

Kent nodded. "Gay marriage?"

"Internationally recognized."

"Male, females, and . . . ?"

"Mamales and Fales – respectively indicating a male would surgically became a female and female, through surgery, becomes male. Though, many insist on being called male or female and not the new terms."

"I see," Kent said. "Wow, maybe I should spend the day looking at TV. Would you recommend I start with the News?"

"No, sir. I would not."

Kent asked. "Because?"

"Not of any value to you comprehending the world. I have lined up a selection of documentaries, movies, TV series, news footages that would be better. I can have Prax bring you classic popcorn and a glass of white wine for your enjoyment. There will be various snacks throughout the day."

Becky leaned into Kent. "It's been a long time since I've been to the movies. Let's spend the day watching what Mike has cooked up."

Kent turned to Becky and stared her in the eye. He bit his bottom lip. "You have no plans?"

She shook her head. "I took the entire month off for vacation. It's going on week two now. I couldn't possibly think of a better way to spend time with my . . ." She hesitated and frowned briefly. ". . . with you. If you'd let me." Her expression relaxed. "I really would like to spend the day with you." She looked down.

Kent thought she was going to say 'boyfriend'. He coughed, "Then a day of leisure we will spend." Then he frowned. "There is something I want to remember, but can't."

"George used to say the same thing. He mentioned Kevin talked about the memory gaps, too."

"And they were told?"

"The same thing. The process was not perfect. It could have been a corrupted data stream, it could have been a perfect data transfer, but you and everyone else's brains are not identical to Prime's brain, which would support uniqueness."

Kent thought about that as he walked to the front row. "I suppose. But I'd think we'd not remember more."

Becky sat in one of the chairs closest to the isle. "Maybe that's the main question there. How would you guys know what was missing if you can't remember it? I can't remember my first cell phone number, for instance."

Kent took a chair opposite Becky's. He nodded, "True, but you remember you had a cell phone number. I remember I forgot something, but can't remember what I forgot. If I were positive I memorized a credit card number and then later forgot the number I could be confident it is somewhere in my head to remember. But some of these gaps are almost like . . . gaps." He frowned, "Like intentional cuts."

"Maybe buffered data forced in a wait state and when the flow restarted there was a space between to the two points?"

"You guys talked often about this?"

Becky slowly nodded, "Some. I bounced lots of ideas off George and vice versa."

Kent squinted his eyes. "Did George leave any memories for me?"

Silence hung awkwardly in the air.

Mike finally said, "Yes, he did. I wasn't going to mention anything until you've had some weeks' time getting used to being you."

"How come?"

"George recorded a substantial amount of himself."

Becky's eyes widened. "That I didn't know."

"Yes, ma'am. About 8,652 hours, 2 minutes, and 39 seconds."

"Almost a year's worth!" Kent exclaimed.

"Yes, sir." Mike said. "He'd hope the option would come up sooner than later."

"Other than you hoping I get some me time in, what are the dangers?"

Mike remained silent for about three minutes.

Becky said nothing and seemed surprised that Kent waited just as long. She learned long ago the art of shutting mouth, especially with Mike. When he was ready to talk he would. George had some patience, just enough she thought. Kent had more. She was about to ask Mike was he still "thinking" when he said.

"Personality overlapping."

Kent asked, "The memory transference from another clone is that pervasive?"

Mike replied, "In this case, it may be. George recorded so much of his memory that his prejudices, of which you may not have formed yet or may have a different view, might overlap or replace yours. Replacement is not what I'm worried about."

Kent nodded, "Overlapping. It may cause some schisms and psychoses. That's not good."

Becky said, "Mike, did George make a visual record of what he backed up?"

"He did not."

"Any way to only send it to short term memory?"

Mike answered, "Undetermined."

"Dreams, what about making the memories dreams?"

"Undetermined."

Kent said, "Seriously? In twenty years none of the

Petes, Kevin, or George thought this through? It must have come up before."

Mike answered, "It has, sir."

Becky spoke up, "George and I had many nights of discussing this, but I thought it was all thought experimenting and hypothetical."

"Mike, could we take a section of George's memory and encode it as a dream. I don't think I need all of it at once."

"Undetermined if fragmented memories could work as a dream. There would be no referenced beginning or end."

Kent nodded, "That's the point. Just like dreams. Yeah, sometimes we all dream in a beginning middle and end, but often times we don't remember the beginning or the first of the beginning. This could be one of those times. If I retain it, good. If not, no harm."

"But, sir. The stream would have been inserted into you conscious. There is no precedence in this. We will be working with memories duplicated to the neuron impulse."

"Mike, I'm surprised at you."

"How so, sir."

"I have most of Pete's memory. Remember."

"I do remember, sir. However, please let me point out that you began with a blank slate. The process imprinted over a brain that had no exterior stimuli. Once transference is done, we cannot undo."

"Let's look at this logically. George would be methodical and exact. I think he would give this careful thought and record what was important. I think he would avoid recording opinionated memories."

Becky thought about that, "Kent, George used the

term 'Repeater Loop Cycle' often."

"Oh, that. It is possible he could've recorded a memory that looped multiple times, in his mind, during the recording process. It is quite natural." He looked up at the ceiling. "Mike, how did George record the memories?"

At that moment, Prax stepped close.

Kent visibly jumped. The Android had silently walked up on him. "Jesus, Prax! Can't you make some noise when you walk up on me?"

"No, sir. I will not."

Kent frowned for a second, then his expression turned light. His brows raised and he smiled. "Understood. I'll just have to be more aware of my surroundings, then?"

"Very good, sir. Being aware of one's surroundings is never a bad idea."

Kent was finally getting it. "Prax, may I ask you a personal question?"

"You may ask, sir?"

"And, please do not be offended. I'm new here."

Prax expression never changed.

"Your CPU, is it in your head or are you accessing your cognitive process off base?"

Prax remained silent for a few moments. This one was curious he thought. He was created by Pete Prime, but this one interested him. For no particular logical reason he could compute Prax decided to give this one time to grow. "My CPU is in my head. So is my reasoning logic and everything that makes me . . . me."

Kent nodded. "Extraordinary."

"If you say so, sir. Extraordinary. May I ask you a personal question?"

"Of course!"

"And, please do not be offended. You're new to me."
Kent smiled and nodded.

"How do you know you are you and not Pete Prime?"

"That is a very good question. I feel like me . . ."

". . . feel, sir?"

Kent nodded, "You and George never talked about feelings?"

"No, sir"

"Seriously?"

"Seriously." The android replied. "However, Ms. Becky and I have talked."

Becky injected, "Kent, Prax really thinks. Don't let him fool you."

Prax continued, "I understand the definition. I understand the process. I was not created with stimuli in mind. I cannot 'feel'."

Kent nodded. "I am so, so sorry."

"Sorry, sir? Ms. Becky said the same thing."

"Would you like to 'feel'?"

Prax answered immediately, "Feel?"

"Yes. Would you like to feel happy, sad, jealous, anger, envy, pride, afraid? Would you like to feel those and more?"

"No, sir. I would not."

"And that is because?"

"They are very unproductive."

"Agreed. Totally a waste of time . . . sometimes. But not always."

Prax said, "Do you have some insight to add to the conversations Ms. Becky and I have had?"

Kent shrugged, "Maybe. Maybe what I'll mention has been covered already. May I try?"

"Of course, sir. I can always hear what you have to say. Anything else would be rude."

"Prax, I like you."

"Which is completely irrelevant to the discussion at the moment."

Kent smiled, "Really? Okay, before we get started I have a mathematical question for you."

"Yes, sir."

"And it relates to emotions."

"Yes, sir."

"Hypothetically I have a piece of string that when folded in half gives equal sides of 11 inches . . . um, we still use inches right?"

"We do, sir."

"Good. If I tie the ends together I get a string, when folded in half that is 10 inches. Suppose I make a rectangle out of the string with one side 1 inch and the other side 9 inches. The area should be 9 square inches, correct."

Prax hesitated a second. "Yes, sir. Nine square inches."

Kent said, "Now, suppose I make a square, with the same string, with the sides 5 inches each."

"Yes, sir."

"I now have 25 square inches, correct."

"Correct, sir."

"Prax, that's the point."

"I don't understand, sir."

"The length after tying the knot never changed. Logic says that it is completely plausible. We are dealing with potentials, relatives, and variables, not absolutes. Simple algebra." He paused.

Prax said, "And what would . . . I presume you would

use the word emotion? . . ."

Kent nodded.

"What would emotion say?"

"Whoa."

Prax paused for a moment and slowly said, "Whoa, sir?"

"Whoa. As in 'I didn't see that coming,' 'wow,' 'mind blown'."

Prax remained silent for a few seconds before he turned and walked toward the door.

Becky watched amused. With her arms akimbo she smiled.

Kent smiled. "But, Prax, we aren't finished yet."

Prax kept walking, but said, "Sir, please allow me a moment to ponder over our brief conversation."

"Of course, Prax. Of course."

Becky said, "Interesting."

Kent turned toward her. "How so?"

"Not even George could do that."

"Make an Android ponder?" He lightly laughed.

Becky nodded. "At the most, we've been able to make him pause for a few seconds, but he almost always came back with a rebuttal or counter argument. You left him speechless."

Kent rolled that through his mind. "I considered all the arguments I would have used, which by default George and all the others would have used and thought of something I would never have used. I mean, one of my college math teachers presented that to the class once. I thought 'wow!'."

Prax walked to his holding station and locked in.

Mike said, "Interesting argument."

Prax replied, "Very interesting. Unexpected."

Mike said, "Indeed."

After several minutes Prax replied, "Whoa."

Chapter 9

Rick Pearl held a tablet in his hand. On the screen was a slightly hazy image of Dr. Pete Walker. The image showed him behind some large wooden crates. He was wearing some kind of backpack. Rick squinted and rubbed his forehead. It certainly looked like Dr. Pete Walker, but that was impossible. Dr. Walker died years ago. He should know. He was there. Dr. Walker agreed to an interview, but only in public. They met at the then new outdoor restaurant Slaa'mcho. It was 1:30 pm, the sky was clear, traffic was light. He had just asked Dr. Walker about his recent departure from Forever Life, Inc., when, out of nowhere, a car plowed through the sidewalk crowd. The car struck Walker dead center. Rick suffered a broken arm and leg. Rehab took him nearly a year. Walker lost his life. The driver had been an elderly man in his 80s. His car, unimportant, had been a tenth his age, but he let maintenance lapse. The brakes failed and at that moment, karma was paid by a dozen people. Scores of other's had been spared the burden of payment.

Barbara Tipper sat at the desk next to Rick's.

He sighed and sat back.

"The Forrest case?" She asked.

He nodded. "It's maddening," he leaned forward, "Pete Walker died almost fifteen years ago, yet here he is . . . again." He turned the tablet so that Barbara can see the image.

"A clone?" She laughed.

He shrugged. "A clone." He said more to himself and frowned. "He wouldn't have been able to do it in this country."

"You sure about that? Madonna cloned herself. And, so did Michae . . ."

"Rumors and not in this country." He interrupted.

"Money, power, remember?"

He nodded. "The UK. If he did."

Barbara said, "Well, are you sure it's Walker?"

He slowly shook his head. "It looks like him. It'll be a few more days for Forensics to finish." He pulled the top drawer open and grabbed a blue and yellow wrapped piece of gum with red writing. He untwirled the ends and slipped out a piece of pink bubblegum. The drawer was full of open wrappers. He fished for several more unopened wrappers, looked at the trashcan, and decided to not throw the empty wrappers away. Not yet. He needed the reminder that he was eating too much gum. It would have been alright if he spat the stuff out after chewing away the flavor, but he just couldn't. It was a habit he started as a kid. Chew, chew, bite a small piece off, swallow it. Over and over again until it was all gone.

Barbara watched as Rick, her partner, popped a piece of bubblegum in his mouth. Smoking was a bitch. Kicking the habit was bitchier. She marked her desk calendar with a line next to lots of other lines and slashes. She was counting the number of times he chewed gum, which in his case swallowed.

Rick slid his finger across the screen. Another image showed. "Pete" ran through a door way. Several guards had walked out earlier. "Barbara, anything yet on internal cameras?"

Barbara typed at her desktop computer. The monitor was about 24 inches wide and rested flat on her desk. Rick liked the monitor upright. Barbara liked her's flat. Several text messages popped up on the screen. "Nothing yet . . ." One text message read, "Retired Keycard used." She tapped out a command. "Interesting." She queried the computer further. Absentmindedly she said, "How can an expired keycard still work?"

Rick looked up, "Got something?"

"Maybe." She scrolled through several images. There. Pete Walker. "No way!"

Rick stretched his neck for a better look. He smiled. "Now you think there's something hinky going on?"

She sent the images and computer text dialog to her printer. Several 4x6 thin white plastic cards slid out of her printer and slid into a tray. Various QVCs, RUL codes and contact morph bumps covered the surface of each card. She slipped the cards into thin open slots on her tablet.

Rick said, "I think we need to take a trip out to the Forever Life Building."

She nodded.

Rick reached over to his desk phone. He said, "The Captain."

Seconds later the small screen lit to a grizzled graying man with thick eyebrows. "Kovik, here."

Rick faced the small monitor, "Captain. Tip and I

need to make a run to the Forever Life Building."

Kovik scowled. "You do?"

Rick nodded. "Questions, sir. Questions."

Kovik tapped at something off-screen. A few seconds later, "Approved. Micro Forensics is still there. Tell the guard 'Code Foxtrot Oscar'. Forrest started leaning on the Commander and City Council about an hour ago. We got another five hours to get what we can." He gave an intense stare into the screen.

Rick gave him a mocking intense stare back, "Understood, sir."

Kovik snorted, "Out."

Rick leaned back and smiled.

Barbara said, "You better cut that out. One day the old man is gonna come down here and kick your ass . . ."

". . . until that time comes I can continue practicing." He laughed softly. He checked his ID badge, gun, wallet, and keys.

Barbara said, "My turn to drive."

"Really?

"Really."

"Alright. Let me get my helmet and kevlar."

"Fuck you," she spat.

Rick smiled, "You keep threatening. Put up or shut up." He laughed.

Barbara stuck her tongue out.

"Insult or offering?"

She shook her head, "I keep falling for that silly shit of yours," and walked out the door to the garage.

Rick smiled and followed. Tip was stone gay, which made teasing her all the more fun. Once they did kiss. It was kind of weird. Both tried again, admitted it felt good, but decided partners first was better. Neither mentioned it again.

***

Forrest had accepted the message from Captain Kovik. He was tempted to deny further visitation. It would have been all on principle if he had, of course, but to what end? He acknowledged the message and replied with "Granted". Forever Life was on the verge of making hundreds of billions of dollars. This setback was at best a nuisance. Acting like a legitimate investigation was counterproductive to business as usual would drop share points. He had the stockholders to consider. So, by his grace he allowed the police to do their job. He knew what they would find and the firestorm and maelstrom of rumors, speculation, and acquisitions would begin again. Forever Life stocks would drop . . . for a time and then rebound. That in and of itself was good. He'd sell some of his shares during freefall and buy at the bottom. But the issue was Walker. His clones were bites on his ass that never seemed to fade away. Every few years a bite would break skin and the pain would be sharp. Other times the bite felt more like a nibble and tickled. This bite went deep into the hypodermis and drew blood.

Forrest sat behind his desk while the two detectives were led in. He motioned for them to sit in the only two chairs in front of his massive oak desk. "Would you like something to drink?" Forrest asked.

Rick, not one to pass up an offer to taste good booze said yes. Barbara said water.

"Anything in particular, Detective? Troy is very adept."

"Cognac?"

Forrest's assistant, Troy, nodded and walked over to a wet bar at one end of the office. He made Mr. Taylor's usual – Gin and tonic with one Gaeta olive speared by a tooth pick. He dropped several cubes of ice into a frosted glass and topped it with water. For Rick's drink he poured a generous amount of Louis the XIII into a short glass. He added a bit of club soda and some bitters. He carried the drinks on a tray and handed them out when he reached Forrest's desk.

Forrest nodded. "I'll buzz you when the good detectives are ready to leave."

Troy nodded and walked out with the tray underneath his arms.

Rick sipped his Cognac mix and savored the smooth burn down his throat.

Forrest sipped at his drink, "So Detectives, how may I be of service?"

Barbara watched Forrest and noted he was almost too cool. His breathing was steady at 10 breaths per minute. She could not tell his pulse but she figured it was low. His bio showed that he ran quarter marathons five days a week and swam Olympic like performances on the weekends in his super-sized pool. He was the fifteenth richest man in the world, but didn't overly flaunt it. He paid his workers well, gave great bonuses at the end of the year, and seldom threw parties. He lived alone – that is as much alone as a billionaire and a mansion full of servants who fulfilled his needs twenty-four seven. He never married, but dated some of the most famous men and women Hollywood produced.

"Clones."

Forrest never blinked. "Clones are illegal in this country?"

"Have you seen the video feeds from today?"

"I haven't, but you have?"

Rick nodded. "It's very interesting. In one frame there is an image of the suicide bomber. . ."

"Bastard." Forrest spat.

Barbara wasn't sure if it was anger toward the bomber or what it cost him in delays. She instinctively knew it wasn't for loss of life.

Barbara pulled a 4x6 plastic sheet from her tablet. She handed it to Forrest. He placed the sheet face down on a spot on his desk. The image lit up on his monitor. Clearly it was an image of Pete Walker. And of himself before he made changes. He passed the sheet back to Barbara. "It looks like Pete, but it is not him."

Rick said, "How do you know?"

"Because I oversaw Pete's burial myself. Pete was my brother . . ."

Rick nodded. Twins. Separated at birth, which he never really bought into. Pretty rare to have a twin that was exact in height. There was not one copy number variant. Not one. And that was statistically never going to happen. But everyone played alone. Some in the news media hinted at it, but no one really pushed the issue. The far right didn't nor did the far left. But everyone knew the Walkers were the reason why Congress had passed a rare bipartisan bill preventing full bodied cloning in America. Parts and organs could be cloned, but not a whole person to full term. "Yes, sir, I understand. But, clearly this individual looks like Pete Walker, he . . ."

"Can't be explained," Forrest said.

Rick took a sip from his glass and decided not to push it. "Do you know your enemies personally?"

Forrest paused in mid thought. Of course he did. One can't be as rich and powerful as he was without having to crush one or two lives. Climbing the ladder involves stepping on rungs. Who's to say how easy it is to avoid the fingers of others wrapped around said rungs. "Detective, I have plenty of enemies. Rivals, too. Pharmaceutical drugs is a billion annually earned business. Forever Life, Inc. by its very nature survives by the attritions of others. So, the list of people and corporate entities who hate me and the company is probably very long."

Rick nodded, "Is it possible to get a list of names, addresses, and numbers or companies who may hate you enough to send in a suicide bomber?"

Forrest thought for a moment. He pressed an intercom button on his desk. "Troy, please prepare a PDS sheet from the CiTC folder."

A few moments later Troy walked in holding a thin white plastic 4x6 card. He handed it to Barbara. She slipped the PDS into her tablet and grunted. "No kidding, very long."

Rick said, "The keycard that had been used was Pete Walker's expired keycard." He let that hang in the air.

Forrest refused to take the bait. "Interesting."

"That's all you have to say?"

Forrest nodded, "What would you like me to say?"

Both men remained silent for a time.

Barbara cleared her throat and started getting up, "Mr. Taylor, thank you for your time. If you don't mind we'd like to make a pass at the damaged floor."

Forrest slowly broke eye contact with Rick, "Why of course." He look toward Rick, "I'll have Troy escort you."

Rick got up slowly, nodded, and said, "Thank you."

Forrest gave him a nod and pressed the intercom button. "Troy, please escort the good detectives to the RDC."

The door opened. Troy waited for Barbara and Rick to reach him.

After the detectives left Forrest swung his chair toward to the large window. He stared at his reflection. "Even after all these years, Brother, you torment me. May you give me rest from sins we both committed?"

Rick and Barbara followed Troy to the elevator that would take them to RDC. Several guards snapped to attention as the three walked passed.

"Excuse me, Troy. May I ask you a question?" Rick spoke.

Troy gave him a side glance, but didn't answer.

Rick smiled. "I'll take you're not saying 'no' as a 'yes'."

Troy continued to walk.

"Do you like working for Mr. Taylor?"

Troy stopped. Turned to face Rick fully. "I am paid extraordinarily well. The benefits are dream like. Mr. Taylor is not a tyrant. What do you think?"

Rick said, "Fair enough. Did you know his brother Pete Walker?"

Troy started walking to the elevator. "Not personally."

The doors parted and all three entered.

Troy leaned into a retina scanner and said, "RDC"

Several lights on the elevator wall panel flashed

green.

Barbara felt the smooth acceleration as the elevator descended the distance to the RDC. She counted 20 seconds. Must be about 80 stories down, which was about right given the visible damage observed from the ground. Forrest's office was near the top, the damage was about a third from the bottom. The doors opened and Troy lead the two out, down a long corridor to an area that was akin to a warzone. Twisted and mangled metal poles jetted out randomly. Concrete walls with large holes seemed to be on the verge of collapse filled the landscape. Bright yellow Caution tape stretched across an opening to the side. All three stepped underneath the tape and walked toward a small knot of three individuals hunched over a particularly dark spot – there were a dozen scattered throughout the room along the floor and walls. This spot was about twenty feet wide. The Micro Forensics team collectively looked up as Troy, Barbara and Rick approached. Rick flashed his badge. The team went back to work.

One said, "Not flash bang." His nametag read "Thompson".

The second one, female, was wearing a helmet of sorts. Her name tag read "Smekhov". Two large goggle linked lens protruded from the front. Rick thought "Steampunk", changed his mind. "Animapunk" would had fit better. The third person, male, was holding a tablet out in front of him. His name tag read "Anosov".

Smekhov said "found it. Spec shows Pent."

Anosov slid his finger across the tablet screen. He whispered "pent". The screen brightened then dimmed to show a chart of colored lines. He nodded. "High grade." The screen changed again. "Res in down to a millapic on that grain."

Smekhov whispered something into her helmet mike. "It's pure."

Anosov nodded, "Surpasses Chi grade."

Rick frowned, "And that means?"

Thompson looked up, "Means we're fucked if this stuff can be made at high volume. We'll have a better estimate later but this one big black spot was caused by a thumbnail sized device."

Silence hung between them.

Thompson continued, "The walls were ten feet thick, reinforced with high tensile-compression strength composites."

To underscore his words wind blew in from several gaping holes, at various points along the outside walls, and stirred up loose paperwork that survived the blast. Troy rushed to collect the papers before the wind carried them outside.

"It's a wonder the main blast hadn't taken out the floors above and below us."

Rick said, "Main blast?"

Anosov said, "These black spots are probably caused by those thumbnail grenades. The extreme damage we see around us was caused by one large, final blast."

Rick thought a bit.

Barbara ventured, "So our bomber gained access into this room, tossed around 'grenades' . . ." she spread her hands out and made quotes signs in the air, ". . . and then blew himself up?"

All three shrugged. Smekhov took off her helmet. Blond hair unfolded onto her shoulders. "Don't know . . . yet. P&R finished mapping a few hours ago. Once a GramVid is created we'll be able to get a probable sequence of events. Give'em 40 hours, maybe more."

Rick asked, "And your finds?"

The three looked at one another, faced Rick and Barbara, and said in unison, "24 hours. We need sleep and nourishment." All three slowly smiled simultaneously.

Rick and Barbara thought that moment a bit creepy. Troy stopped in mid step. A piece of paper with burnt edges flew passed his face, reached the outside and blew off in the distance.

Thompson said, "Well, we do need sleep."

Rick nodded and took a step back.

Barbara followed and Troy cleared his throat. "Detectives, anything else I may be able to help you with?"

Rick said, "Can you tell us . . ." His voice trailed off as he noticed about a dozen men in dark suits standing throughout the room. He hadn't noticed them when he first entered, or even when he looked around earlier. "How long have they been here?"

Without looking Troy answered, "They've always been here."

Rick frowned.

Smekhov said, "It is true. It's Forever Life Security."

The three looked at one another again and in unison said slowly, "They watch over us." The identical smiles returned.

Rick and Barbara paused.

Troy said, "If I am not needed I'll leave you to finish up. One of the Security Units will escort you to the lift when you are done."

Barbara looked up to where Troy was pointing at. She finally noticed Security. Over a dozen scattered throughout the floor pressed closed to the many shadows across the room. "Now that's creepy."

Rick cleared his voice. "Hey, Troy! Wait up. We're done." Rick turned and started walking to the door. "I'll catch up with you guys sometime tomorrow." He almost bumped into Barbara as both walked a bit too fast.

Thompson and the others faced the retreating group and in unison said, "That would be nice. See you tomorrow." Their voice combined to hit a resonating discord. He watched as Troy, Rick, and Barbara walked out. All the while a half dozen security units monitored their progress. Once the door closed Thompson let out a laugh. "That was the funniest shit we ever pulled off."

Anosov and Smekhov joined him.

Smekhov said, "Did you see when Troy stopped and that piece of paper nearly hit him in the face?"

Anosov replied, "I had a hard time NOT laughing. Guys we're gonna have to make up more of these."

Chapter 10

Rick and Barbara pulled into a parking spot outside The Lo'tion Diner – it was often mispronounced as 'lotion', but the owner pronounced it 'low-she-own'. It was a local restaurant that specialized in home comfort food with a retro style built back in the double-aught ages. Barbara turned the cruiser off. "You've been pretty quiet."

Rick shifted in his seat. "It's all a lie, Barb. Forrest fed us shit and I'm almost certain the bomber was Walker or a Walker clone."

"How would a clone get into this country?"

"Like everyone else. False cards . . ."

"But what about retina scan?"

"New eyes. Even in this country, we'll use cloned organs and limbs."

She nodded. "Okay, supposing it was a clone, the question is why a clone?"

"Why? Barb! Think about it. The ultimate suicide bomber. An unlimited supply!"

"An expensive supply. More expensive than a Titan Hawk cruise missile."

Rick had to concede that. "Yeah, but almost untraceable."

"Nothing's untraceable these days."

Rick laughed, "I did say 'almost'?"

Barbara's voice took on a serious tone. She turned her upper half to face Rick. "If we follow your thinking then what you are suggesting is epic."

He nodded. "No less. But I've still got this nag hanging on my back."

Barbara lifted her chin up and she frowned.

"Why Walker? Why Forever Life?"

"Forrest, that's why." She said.

Rick cocked his head to one side. "Forrest?"

"Is a clone."

"Barb! That's bull . . ." He stopped in mid-sentence. "It was the reflex."

Both laughed.

"But, seriously, "Rick said, "Who would send a Pete clone?"

Barbara thought a few seconds. She thought the answer was totally obvious. "Pete Walker."

"Pete!"

"Yeah. You got this lost twin brother thing going on in the past. Like out of nowhere, there he is. First, oddity. Then the question about birth certificates. Number two. Then, the delivery staff. All claim faulty memory, but all enjoying surprisingly improbable luck with the lottery. And . . ."

"Okay, okay, I'm impressed. I hadn't known you had an interest in the Walker Conspiracy?"

"Ha! Who hadn't! That fueled my young teenage mind. All my friends were into it. That's all we talked about."

Rick scratched the bottom of his chin. He reached into his jacket pocket and pulled out his gum. He unwrapped the wrapper and popped the gum in his mouth.

Barbara automatically said, "Don't swallow."

Rick automatically retorted, "What do you know about swallowing?"

"Fuck you!"

"And, you always threaten. Never follow through."

Both laughed.

Barbara said as she opened the car door. "I'm hungry. Stop talking and get out."

Sarah Hill dropped off an order at table two. It was ham cooked well, eggs sunny side up with whites firm, white toast plain and a cup of coffee.

Joe, the restaurant's regular, said, "Thanks Sarah. You free tonight?"

She laughed and walked off.

Rick and Barbara walked through the door.

Rick called out, "Hey Sarah."

Sarah looked up, turned from wiping off a table and smiled. Rick and Barb were her favorites. They tipped very well. She walked over and greeted the two. "I got a table cleaned off." She gestured toward the table she finished cleaning.

Rick sat on one side of the booth.

Barbara sat at the other end.

Sarah asked, "The usual or something else?"

Rick visibly relaxed and said, "Pastrami, rye, the works, no pickle." He hesitated and thought for a moment. "Give me a Bell's, please."

Barbara said, "Now?"

Rick shrugged and nodded. "Why not. You're

driving." His smile was broad.

Barbara gave him an evil eye. Her frown was deep. "I'll have my usual, with water."

Sarah nodded and jotted down the orders. She liked the detectives and had sexual fantasies about both. Rick fulfilled her sense of normalcy while Barbara took care of a carefree and wild side. She dreamt of being bedded by the two. They seemed fun and clearly the chemistry between the two worked. They teased openly and genuinely liked and respected one another. She knew Rick was straight and Barbara was gay, of which really meant nothing except she could have the best of both worlds. She nodded, "Coming right up." She turned and walked away to place the order with the head cook. She came out and headed to another table. A minute later she had their order placed.

Rick caught Barbara staring at the rear end of a retreating Sarah. He leaned over to her. "You'd do her wouldn't you?"

Barbara gave Rick a coy smile. "Maybe, maybe not. I've seen the way she looks at you."

"Me?!?"

"Seriously, you never noticed?"

He pulled out a bubblegum, unwrapped it, and popped it into his mouth. "I'm a regular guy. I don't notice those subtle female things. I'm . . ."

". . . divorced because of it."

"Gut punch. Not fair."

Just then Sarah stepped out into the dining area. Had a glass of water and a bottle of Bell's. She figured Rick wanted to drink straight from the bottle.

Rick looked up as she placed the bottle in front of him. He smiled. 'How did she know,' he thought.

Sarah swept some hair that had drifted in front of her eye behind her ear. She smiled back. A second later she heard Barbara cough. She realized she hadn't placed the glass down yet. "Sorry."

Barbara smiled, "How's it been, Sarah? Anything new?"

Sarah gushed, "Just working. Nothing new, no, wait. We did have someone from the station take samples on Mel's food. She asked him to cook everything on the menu. Mel was tickled. It took about five hours but he did it, she paid full price and left a wonderful tip."

Barbara said, "Really? She leave a name or card?"

Sarah shook her head, "Her name tag read Smekhov."

Rick laughed, "Probably one of those spooky projects they got going on in the lab."

Barbara answered, "Probably. With those guys you can't tell."

Sarah politely nodded.

Barbara noticed and gave Rick a light tap on his shin with her foot.

He gave her the evil eye. "Hey, Sarah, is that a new do?"

Sarah blushed, "Since the last time you saw me, yeah."

He totally bullshitted and hit target. "Very nice."

Several seconds ticked by. Barbara kicked Rick's shin harder.

"Hey, Sarah, what do you do these days when not working?"

A smile formed on her face and she blushed lightly. "Not much. Sometimes I catch a movie. You know they redid The Bridge a few weeks ago?"

"I heard. I had been meaning to go, but . . . you know . . ."

She nodded, "Yeah, me, too."

Mel yelled out from back, "Order!"

Sarah frowned and looked back. "Foods ready, be back."

Once Sarah was out of earshot Rick leaned over, "Stop kicking me will ya?"

Barbara smiled, "Smooth moves Romeo. Like, 'I had been meaning to go . . . umm, d'oh . . . but . . . umm, d'oh . . . you know . . .'" She laughed.

"You can do better? I didn't just want to come on strong?"

Barbara smiled, "I know. And, I'm sure she appreciated it."

Rick nodded.

"Just ask her out. She'll either say yes or no."

"All that easy for you?"

"Rick, trust me on this."

He was about to reply when Sarah came out with their order.

She placed Barbara's Mushroom Florentine Crepes down first.

"Sarah, are you free tonight?"

She nearly dropped his plate. Instinctively, Rick reached out to save his meal. Sarah recovered in time and neatly placed it in front of him. She cleared her throat, "As a matter of fact, I am free." She waited.

Barbara kicked Rick in the shin.

Rick winced and forced a smile. "Wanna see a movie or something?"

She smiled and nodded. "Yes, I would."

Ricked seemed surprised. All that easy he thought.

Damn you Barb. "What time do you get off tonight?"

"Eight? We're a bit short handed, so I have to pull time and a half." She suddenly frowned. "Is that too late?"

Rick smiled and half closed his eyes. "Eight would be just fine. You wanna met there? Or should I pick you up?"

She replied, "We can meet there. I don't wanna inconvenience you . . ."

"Not at all!"

". . . in front of the ticket office? 8:30?"

He nodded. "Sounds good . . ."

Mel yelled, "Order!"

Sarah smiled, turned and walked into the kitchen.

Barbara kicked Rick.

"Goddamnit woman. Kick me in the shin again and I'm stomping that little man in the boat's head in.

So she did it again, but harder.

He reached down and rubbed his shin.

Barbara squinted and stuck her tongue out. "Care to rephrase that?"

Chapter 11

"Prax?"

"Yes, sir?"

"I was hoping to satisfy a curiosity, if you don't mind?"

"Mind, sir?"

Kent nodded, "Yes. It's about emotions."

Prax turned to fully face Kent. His blank expression was unnerving. He remained silent.

"Are you able to change your expression?"

"Yes, sir, I am."

Kent smiled, "And you choose to show a face devoid of expression?"

"Yes, sir."

"I see. If you were inclined to pick an expression, which one would it be?"

"Sir, why would I be inclined to select an expression?"

"One, it lets those around you know what kind of mood you are in. Kind of like a warning or a welcome."

"I see," said Prax. "And you would like me to show an expression?"

Kent nodded. "It would be nice. I know you were created, but I also know you are an independent thinker. Are you self-aware?"

Prax paused a moment. "Is it necessary for me to be so, sir?"

Kent slowly shook his head and pursed his lips into a frown. "Not at all. But the expression, Prax? Which one would you show?"

Prax stood for several minutes.

Kent waited. "Would you like to talk it out? You know, discuss the subtle differences."

"Annoyance, sir."

"Pardon?" Kent replied.

Prax turned and started walking away.

"Annoyance is it?" Kent was not surprised.

"Yes, sir, annoyance."

Kent laughed softly. "Why annoyance?"

Prax stopped and turned around. His expression slowly changed. "Sir, do I really have to explain?"

Kent smiled. "I think not. Thank you, Prax."

Prax resumed walking. He stepped out the room to finish his daily chores.

"Mike," Kent spoke at the ceiling.

"Yes, sir? How may I be of assistance?"

"Radio, is radio still played?"

"It is, sir. I can feed the audio into the auditorium."

"Thank you, Mike. I'd like that."

Hours later . . .

Kent sat in the dark listening to a radio broadcast. The main screen was off, but Mike piped the audio through the main speakers.

Becky walked into the darkened theater and sat down next to him.

"I can't believe you still have radio." He said.

She nodded. "Mostly the fringe, conspiracy theorists, and church groups crowd the waves. There's a few public stations, but not many left. Because of the Universal Radio Access Spectrum Spread Law of 2020 anyone can be a radio station. Filing fee is low and you are allowed a broadcast range of 2 kilometers. Shortwave is off limits, but Low power is allowed."

"Yeah. I listened to Sesame Street. Go figure. Sesame Street on the radio."

Becky reached out and felt Kent's fingers. She gave them a squeeze.

"I saw the news, the documentaries, hours of bullshit. Then the radio, and . . ."

She held her breathe.

"The great economic divide never closed."

Even though he couldn't see her she nodded anyway. Tears started welling up in her eyes. Her George talked like that. His voice held a resonance like sorrow. But Kent seemed to be affected more.

"Becky, twenty years of political fighting. We lost the space race because of it. We suffered the greatest amount of brain drain the world witnessed because of political religious hijackers. It took four years under a conservative President, with a majority House and Senate to tear down sixty years of innovation, ingenuity, inspiration." He shook his head. "Sorry, you lived through all of this. None of this is new to you." He sighed. "I must sound pathetic."

"Not in the least. We think alike . . ."

"You mean, you and George think alike."

Becky bit down a flash of anger. "No, you and I think alike. You are not George."

"I'm cut from the same mold, I'm . . ."

"Not like George." She said it a little too loud. "Look, Kent, if you were like anyone it'd be Pete."

"Pete?!?"

"George had six years to diverge from Pete prime. You've only been here a few days. You add that up." She let his hand go, got up and walked out. This is the part she was going to hate. The self-doubt and questioning. George had a hard time shaking off the specter of Kevin. Kent, now alone, couldn't stop thinking of what Becky said. '. . . if you were like anyone it'd be Pete.' This was going to nag at him for a while.

Mike said, "Sir, shall I continue?"

"What do you think I should do, Mike?"

"Pardon, sir?"

"I'm asking for your advice. What should I do?"

There was a long pause. "Do nothing, sir."

"Nothing?"

"Yes. Nothing."

Kent pondered that for a moment. "Mike, continue, please."

The broadcaster began, "It was written in Genesis 6 that the Nephilim took human females as wives and lovers. The spawned hybrid creatures, half human half fallen angels. As time wore on God decided he had to rid the world of these abominations and all of Earth's wickedness. So, he tasked Noah to build the Ark."

Kent listened bemused. Hadn't the coming invasion happened already? The Nephilim, Greys, Talls, all of them were supposed to reveal themselves to all of humankind. Twenty years ago. "Mike, I'm done with the fringe stuff."

The broadcast stopped.

"Thank you." Kent sat in the darkness and let the

minutes slip into hours. He got up looking for Becky. He had to talk to her. He wanted her thoughts.

Becky sat in the upper Living area looking at pre-recorded shows on a large flat sheet monitor along the wall. George and she purchased the sheet a year ago. She barely watched it, but as of late she was feeling nostalgic.

"Becky."

She turned at the sound of George's . . . Kent's voice.

He rushed to her side. "I need to talk to you."

She was still miffed at Kent, but forced a congenial smile.

"I was thinking about George's memories. The more I think about it, the more I am convinced it's safe."

"But Mike is not sure, if . . ."

"Becky, George had years to think about this. I can't see him or me, not thinking this through. I need to do this."

Becky withdrew her hand.

Kent shifted in his seat, "Becky, I need this. Otherwise, it'll take months, if not years to know enough to do anything about Forever Life."

She nodded and bit her bottom lip.

Kent picked up on the gesture. "There are other things I need to know . . ." his voice trailed off.

"Such as?"

His smile was slight, but he didn't want to give away too much. "Stuff."

"Stuff?"

He nodded.

"You care to elaborate?"

The smile remained on his face, but he said nothing.

Becky stared into his eyes for a moment. Her vision adjusted quickly to the darkness. George would have blinked after 20 seconds.

Kent, to his credit, didn't blink. He needed Becky on this.

"Okay. Mike?"

"Yes, Miss. Becky."

"Prepare the seat, please."

"Yes, ma'am."

***

"You look nice, Sarah," Rick said as he approached her. He was about two minutes late and feeling bad about it.

Sarah blushed. "Thank you. You always look nice."

Rick paused. "Really?"

She nodded, smiled sweetly, and brushed some hair from in front of her eyes. She had most of it bunched up in a ponytail, but almost always she missed some strands, which always drifted and dangled in front of her eyes.

A couple of seconds ticked by as the silence crept into being uncomfortable.

Rick finally cleared his throat and turned to look at what was playing. Nothing too interesting. "Anything in particular you'd like to see? Some of the titles look interesting, but . . ."

Sarah stopped looking at him and glanced at the list of movies. "Yeah, I agree. I'm actually hungry, but, we can do a movie, if you'd like?"

He pursed his lips and slightly shook his head. "Food sounds better. Your pick. I'm game for anything."

Sarah had been serving greasy comfort food all day. She did not want to consume the same. "Japanese?"

Rick smiled, "Kabuki's should be right around the corner."

Her smile was genuine and lovely Rick thought.

He gestured for them to start walking.

They walked in silence, but glancing at one another and being caught each time. Finally, Rick laughed. He stopped and looked at Sarah. They were in front of one of the niche clubs that dotted the promenade. This club's name was "China Bay". At the moment, "Anything Goes," was playing.

She stared him in the eye and suddenly got it. She laughed too and nodded.

Rick held out his hand, not certain if she really understood.

She grabbed it and squeezed lightly. She understood. Tonight was fun night.

Chapter 12

Rick stepped into the office and walked to his desk. Barbara bit her bottom lip and looked distressed. She shook her head the moment she saw him. 'Oh, shit!'

"Barb, what?"

She handed him a printout.

He scanned the paper. "Fuck! Seriously!"

"Seriously."

"No no no no! This is total bullshit! No no no no! I can't believe this. No no no no!" He crushed the printout under his clenched hand and stomped out the door to the elevators.

Barbara followed. "What are you going to do?"

"Blow off some steam. I can't believe this!"

The elevator door opened and he walked in before anyone had a chance to exit. He heard someone leaving the elevator say, "Dumbass. Straight up cracked dumbass." He ignored them. "Research," he spoke out loud.

Barbara jumped in just before the doors closed.

The two rode the elevator the short distance in silence. The doors opened and Rick stomped out. He headed to Lab 51. Thompson, Anosov, and Smekhov were there waiting for him.

"Thompson, what the hell?!?"

The three, in unison, said, "We have something more serious to worry about."

Rick's head snapped back, "WTF! Stop this spooky shit. It creeps me and everyone out."

The three said, "We cannot. This is what we are. This is what we do."

Thompson began, "We are . . ."

Anosov continued, ". . . of the . . ."

Smekhov finished, ". . . body and mind."

Rick's face turned deep red. "I don't have time for this bullshit. What happened with the tests?"

The three said, "You better make time if you want answers." The resonating discord sounded chalkboard scratchy.

Rick tried to stare the three down.

Then, in unison, "Do not believe what you hold in your hand. Calm down, follow us, and learn the truth. Our way or leave and be clueless."

Thompson turned and started walking, Anosov followed close, with Smekhov taking up the rear. Rick and Barbara followed all three into Thompson's office. Once inside, Thompson motioned for everyone to sit around a conference table. The surface of the table was a black smooth reflection of touch screen. He stepped over to his desk and picked up a black sphere the size of his fist. He placed it in the center of the table as he sat down in one of the empty chairs. He waved his right hand inches above the surface and edge nearest him. The lights dimmed.

A double helix appeared in midair. Parts of it were missing. Other parts were coded red.

"Is that the bomber's DNA?" Rick asked.

Thompson waved his hand and rapidly spread his fingers apart. The image focused on a line of text in the relative right corner. It read, 'DNA corrupted. Person unknown. Markers destroyed.'

Rick exclaimed, "WTF!"

Thompson swept his hand across the image several times. Each new image had the same text. 'Markers destroyed.'

Rick's depression deepened with each hand swipe. He shook his head. The best piece of evidence they had. Gone.

Thompson said, "Detective. You haven't been paying attention, have you?"

Rick looked up. "What do you mean?"

Thompson stared him in the eye. "We went through all that theatrics not to have you sit teary eyed in full denial of nothing real."

"I'm not tracking."

In unison the three said, "He is not tracking."

"Can you cut that out? Please?"

In unison, "Do it our way or get out. Our job is done. We can go home now."

Rick opened his mouth several times, only to shut it several more times. He looked over to Barbara for support.

She shrugged.

After a moment he visibly relaxed and seemed to accept what was thrown his way. "I give. Continue, please."

The three said, "Finally, he understands."

Rick cringed. The shit these guys do. He heard how creepy they could be, but to witness it first hand?

"Pay attention, please!" A disjointed chorus exclaimed.

Rick flinched.

Thompson said, "Yes, the DNA had been corrupted, but not by the explosion."

Rick frowned.

Thompson said, "We have a saboteur."

Anosov repeated, ". . . saboteur. . ."

Smekhov ended, ". . . saboteur."

Rick shook his head, "You guys are sick. Sick I say!"

Thompson replied, "That may be so, but here you are . . . basking in it."

All three smiled teeth.

The hair at the back of Rick's neck stiffened and a cold chill traveled the length of his spine.

Thompson continued, "We know who the bomber is . . . was. But the disturbing fact that all, and I mean all, our data had been corrupted points to one thing."

"And that is?" Rick asked.

All three said in unison, "Trust no one . . . except us." All three smiled again.

Barbara smiled. She did like the three, intensely odd at times, but likeable none the less.

"Two questions then," Rick began. "Whose DNA was it and who is the saboteur?"

All three shrugged, "We don't know who the saboteur is . . . yet."

Thompson said, "But the DNA . . ."

Anosov continued," . . . belongs to . . ."

Smekhov finished, ". . . Pete Walker."

Rick exhaled loudly, "I knew it!"

Thompson added, "Mostly."

"Wait, what?" Rick responded.

Smekhov added, "Most of the DNA matches Pete Walker, but there are some differences."

Barbara said, "Like?"

Anosov said, "Of course, this can't be Pete Walker. He died decades ago. So the conclusion was the bomber had to be a clone."

Smekhov continued, "But judging from the variation we discovered this individual could legally be classified as related."

Rick thought on that. "Like brothers?"

All three nodded.

Barbara asked, "Could there be more?"

All three nodded. "No reason there shouldn't be."

Thompson suddenly looked serious, "Detectives, this is a game changer. This Pete Walker . . ." He pointed to the DNA strand floating above the table, ". . . is a way to get around the law. The variation is just that different enough."

"Is there anything you can give us to find who made this Pete Walker?" Rick asked.

All three smiled. The effect was scary.

Thompson said, "You gotta love DNA and the odd nature of explosives."

Rick asked, "How so?"

"We know the other Walker had a backpack on . . ."

Rick nodded. Some of the photo feeds showed that.

". . . and not all backpacks are created equal."

Rick nodded again.

"Because of that we got DNA from all sorts of items. Other Walker used Pent, but the pack had a ceramic back plate."

Rick said, "Okay . . . and?"

All three said, "We are pretty certain the contents

on one of the ceramic fragments is from Other Walker's stomach."

They let the silence linger.

Barbara thought a moment, then suddenly blurted out, "You know what he ate?"

All three said, "About 60% certain. A ChemAY got us all the ingredients, but it was . . ."

Smekhov said, ". . . I . . ."

The three continued, ". . . who got the connection."

Rick frowned. "What connection? How the ingredients are combined?"

She nodded and answered, "A few months ago I started cataloging DNA/Seasoning combinations from prepared foods in restaurants."

"We'd know what he had for his last meal and who made it?"

"Exactly. Dirk had been working a case, which stalled for a few weeks. We knew what the victim ate, but not where. It was a question of whether this particular meal was from a restaurant or prepared at someone's home. I visited about 60 restaurants within a five kilometer radius of the crime scene. I had another 100 to go when we got a hit. Dirk got a new led and within a week arrested the mother. She lied about cooking the meal."

Barbara said, "Amazing."

Smekhov nodded. "It was. I finished cataloging the other 100 and started working out from the station. I had put in a dozen food combos from a local diner. Within two hours I got a hit."

Rick perked up. "Okay then. What did he eat?"

"A Pastrami on Baguette. Mayonnaise and yellow mustard. Fried yam chips with ranch. He had a Bell's.'

"That sounds familiar. What diner?"

All three said in unison, "The Lo'tion."

Rick and Barbara stared at one another for several heart beats. Both laughed. A few seconds later the three joined in. They had a face and knew where he had his last meal. Rick thought, 'They can continue their creepy shit.' His eyes welled up with tears. Best news. Ever.

Chapter 13

Walter Kincaid sat at his desk. It was 2:00 am and his obsession with Forever Life, Inc. was creeping into his personal life. He watched the image of the Forever Life building for the umpteen time. The picture was grainy but good enough to make out the explosion. Mostly glass, fire, smoke, and bodies blew out a narrow horizontal patch the entire length on the building's side. He played the image again as his morbid fascination of seeing violent death increased. The computer finished running its spectrometer analysis on the explosion. Walter watched as a graph of colored lines appeared on the screen. It concluded Pent or something similar, which meant sabotage. 'Mind blowing', he thought. To think that a rival would go to this extreme was beyond comprehension. And for what? Some hundreds of billions of dollars? Must be nice Walter finally concluded. "Must be nice," he said aloud. Then suddenly his computer beeped. It seemed rather loud at this time of night. Walter clicked the Inbox icon. It took several seconds to open, which seemed strange. It never took that long to open. "Holy Fuck!" He said when the first image appeared. He checked the reply field of the email. It read, 'Someone-in-the-know'.

As each image appeared Walter's eyes teared up. Someone-in-the-know handed him his Pulitzer Prize story. He laughed as a man who was about to lose his mind – almost a whisper at first, then within seconds a full belly laugh. He looked at his desk clock. 2:12 am. His Editor, Herb Rochester, wouldn't be in for another six hours. The first thing Walter realized he had to do was verify the images. He needed something to substantiate their validity.

A second email came in.

Walter opened it. "WTF?"

The second email had Security tags and PIXconfirm files for each image. It also contained PDFs and CTXs files of reports, memos, emails, names with addresses, and audio files.

Walter slapped his forehead hard. "Screw the WTF. This is now a What the fuck?!?" He rifled through the files. Sweat formed on his forehead. It ran down passed his eyebrows and stung his eyes. 'Screw this,' he thought. This is too big to wait. He reached for his phone and dialed Herb's number. About 30 seconds later Herb answered.

"What the hell, Walt? Why are you still at work?" He heard a sigh and yawn. "You've got to stop this obsession . . ."

"Herb, I . . ."

"Goddess Walt, this had better be good, or so . . ."

"Herb, Herb, it is good. Beyond good. We're talking Pulitzer for the firm."

Herb coughed, "You said that last time. I had to bat for you after that last blow up."

"I got PIXconfirm files." He counted to ten.

"No shit?"

"Yes shit. When can you get down here?"

"What?!? At this hour?"

"It's that big."

Herb hesitated.

"If this is not the big thing I promise you I'll quit in the morning."

After a moment, Herb said, "You serious?"

"Like a heart attack. I'm saving the files to the Beast."

Walter heard a heavy sigh. "Alright. I'll be there in thirty minutes."

"Good. I'll start running the PIXconfirm audit. Should be done before you get here."

"Alright." Herb clicked off.

Walter took a deep breath and let it out slowly. He started the audit process and waited. He was tempted to listen to the audio files, but decided to wait until Herb got in. He was too scared to go any deeper until he had someone looking over his shoulder. 'Most High Goddess this is big.'

***

Kent slipped the helmet over his head.

Becky said, "You don't have to do this."

He nodded, "I know. Mike start the process, please."

The terminal blinked on and tiny lights danced along the front panel.

Kent took a deep breath and closed his eyes. He felt nothing . . . pain. Burning pain wrapped itself around his head. Hot burning pain squeezed at his temples and he felt bursts of sharp stabs puncturing through his scalp. Then nothing . . . pain lingered a bit. Seconds later it disappeared. He opened his eyes.

Becky watched in horror. Kent's face contorted and twisted in agony. It had only been a few minutes but it felt like an hour. She watched as his face relaxed and he started breathing regularly again. His eyes fluttered open and immediately welled up with tears.

"Are you okay, Kent?"

He stared at her with moist eyes. A large grin appeared and his bottom lip started shaking.

"Kent!" Becky said alarmed.

"I'm okay, Beck."

"You scared me for a moment . . . are you sure, you're okay."

He nodded slowly and his grin faded. "Beck?"

She answered, "Yes?" Then she frowned. "You called me Beck?"

He nodded again.

"How would you . . ."

"I love you." He started crying.

She helped take the helmet off.

Kent tried to stand. His knees buckled and he landed hard on the floor.

Becky knelt beside him, trying to lift him up.

Prax waited patiently to be called for assistance.

Kent finally let Becky help him up. She walked him to one of several chairs in the corner. When they reached the chairs he thrust himself into one of them. He sank several inches and relaxed. 'Best ever,' he thought. "We have to wake the others."

"What?!?"

"We have to wake the others."

"All of them?!?"

He shook his head. His mind racing, "Only most."

Becky stared at Kent. She frowned.

Kent's distance gaze disappeared. His eyes focused on Becky. "Really, I'm okay, but I have to think this through . . ."

"Think what through?"

Prepare, prepare, prepare. "George . . . I can't." Tell her, tell her, tell her. "No, I can't."

"You can't what, Kent?"

Tell her, tell her, tell her. Kent held his breath. Were those his thoughts or George's? Tell her, tell her, tell her.

"Kent, what is going on? Please tell me!"

Tell her, tell her, tell her. Kent let out the air slowly. Tell her, tell her. He took another deep breath, counted to ten, and let that breath out slowly. Tell her. One more breath and he felt in control. "Becky, three years ago George and Forrest met just outside the city . . ."

She gasped.

He nodded, "Forrest had asked George to join him. He admitted that Forever Life had been experimenting with cloning at their UK branch. The process was good and the success rate was about 80%, but he wanted 100%. George said he should have been able to figure it out. He was after all Pete, the Pete Alpha. Forrest shook his head. Memory gaps. One day he knew. The next day he forgot. How? He didn't know. He needed a process that was perfect. He needed a means to break the seven clone limit. George thought about it. I mean he really thought about it. They met a dozen more times. Each time the two talked for hours and exchanged ideas. Forrest gave data about Transgenetics and George passed on cloning tech and memory transference. Then the meetings stopped. George had one last bit of datum to give Forrest and likewise with Forrest to give to George. Neither gave in. George wouldn't budge. Forrest became enraged. They never spoke after that again."

Becky sat in silence for a minute.

Kent let her think. The two had been together during that time and he never told her. George lied to Becky and he was sure she was going through turmoil on forgiving him.

"The one thing I can't do?" Becky finally said.

Kent pursed his lips and waited.

"I can't call him a goddamn son-of-a-bitch!"

Kent nodded slowly. His voice was a whisper. "Yes you can."

Becky frowned at first. Then she realized what Kent was offering. She took a deep breath. "Goddamnit, George! What in the world were you thinking! Forrest could have done all sorts of shit on you and I wouldn't know what had happened to you! You are one thick skulled fuck! Understand me! Hard headed and you make me so mad sometimes! Really mad! Jesus, George! JESUS!!! Why! I hate you! Why! Why . . . ! WHY!"

Then there was silence.

Becky sobbed and turned away from Kent. "I'm sorry."

Kent kept silent.

Becky wiped her eyes and faced Kent. "Aren't you going to say something?"

Kent paused for a few seconds. "Something."

Becky's expression lightened. "That's it? No yelling back? No disagreeing? No anything?"

"I am sorry."

Her surprised look was enough for him to

understand. She had her turn, now it was his.

"Becky, I left you. I am sorry. I never meant to leave you, seriously. I just needed to plant the explosives and get out, but I was trapped. Security androids everywhere. I hadn't anticipated that and I messed up. So, I took out as many as I could and reached the main lab. Forever Life hit a speed bump, but only for a few months. Forrest will start again and Transgenetics will go deeper underground until it is FDA approved. This cannot happen. Please, Becky, forgive me. This is about all of humanity. The future of humankind. Our very existence. Forrest is going to take that away and we cannot let him do that. Never. Ever. Can we let him? Never." Kent felt exhausted. Was that George or was it him talking? Academically, he was the single voice, philosophically . . . ? Philosophically, Kent thought, now there was something to that. 'I think, therefore I am,' was not enough to answer that question. Were his thoughts Pete's, Kent's, George's now? A fusion of two, maybe more? I am Geor . . . no. I am Kent. My name is Kent. I am Kent. I. am. Kent. He believed that. It was good. I am Kent.

Becky stared into his eyes for a long moment. She blinked several times and finally said, "Never. Ever." She then nodded and exhaled.

***

Barbara walked into The Lo'tion first. She caught Sarah's expression. It wasn't disappointment, not quite, then a second later it changed to elation. Barbara looked over her shoulder. Her partner, Rick, had been a few seconds behind her. She understood. Their first date had been good. Rick hadn't lied. Apparently he was a gentleman and gave Sarah a fun time. She smiled and said, "Hey, Sarah!"

Sarah walked over to an empty table and motioned for the two to have a seat.

Rick and Sarah smiled and locked eyes. Barbara coughed, "Do you guys need a room?"

Sarah blushed. "Detective Tipper!"

Barbara laughed. "Please Sarah, I think now is the time to call me Barb."

Sarah looked away and nodded.

Rick said, "Hey, Sarah. You look nice."

"Thank you. Anything special I can get you?" She turned her gaze back to Rick.

He smiled and nodded. "Actually, we're here for two reasons."

Her smile disappeared. "Oh?"

Rick frowned and mentally kicked himself. "Sorry . . ." And he lost his voice.

Barbara smiled. "You two are just too cute." She laughed.

"Barb!" Rick exclaimed.

"Sorry, Sarah. You guys had a good time?"

Sarah blushed, looked down and nodded.

"Good. If Rick fucks up in any way, let me know. I'll kick his ass and set him straight."

Sarah, shocked, looked up.

"Barb! WTF!"

Barbara kicked Rick.

"God damnit, woman, stop with the kicking!"

Barbara laughed. "Sarah, I got your back."

Sarah nervously laughed and looked into Rick's eyes."

He rubbed his shin briskly. Then he noticed Sarah's stare and looked up. He lost himself in her gaze and forgot about the pain. "Sarah . . ."

"Yes," she said.

"Don't listen to her. She's butch and likes to bully people."

Barbara leaned forward, said, "And, your point is?" She leaned back, satisfied she established who the Alpha was.

Sarah smiled, looked at Barbara, brushed some hair behind her ear and looked away. She blushed and hoped Barbara hadn't noticed. "So, Rick, Barb, what can I getcha?"

Rick reached into his jacket pocket and pulled out a hardcopy photo printout. He handed it to Sarah.

"Oh my goodness! Did something happen to George?"

"You know, wait, what? George?"

Sarah nodded. "George Walker. He comes in maybe once a week, sometimes once every two weeks. Tips well, but keeps to himself. Mostly."

Barbara's eyebrow raised.

Sarah continued. She said in a rush of breath, "Is he okay. Please tell me nothing bad happened to him."

Rick cleared his throat. He thought 'damn!' and said, "Um, just an ongoing investigation. His name turned up and we're just gathering information."

Sarah eyed Rick for a few seconds. "Rick, you're holding back on me."

Rick swallowed hard. "No, seriously, we're gathering intel." He forced a smile.

Sarah shook her head. "Mister. Don't give me that."

Both locked stares, not blinking.

Rick found himself wavering. His eyes started drying out.

Barbara coughed and both turned toward her. She smiled as Rick and Sarah rapidly blinked.

Sarah squeezed her eyes shut tightly, thankful for the distraction.

"Sarah," Barbara said, "It is important and we can't say too much about it now. What else do you know about George?"

Sarah took a deep breathe. "He has a girlfriend. Becky's her name. Very pretty."

Rick asked, "Address, maybe?"

Sarah shook her head. "Figured he lived in the area. Never saw a car. When he came in by himself he would sit reading some sort of book."

"He pay by Credit Card?"

"Never. He paid with credits, cash or CashCard."

Barbara asked, "What type of books?"

"He . . ."

"Order!" Mel shouted from the back.

Sarah said, "Hold that thought." She rushed into the back. A moment later she rushed out, stopped at Joe's table, placed the food in front of him and rushed away. Joe was left with his mouth open and a pained look on his face. She stopped in front of Rick and Barbara. Her smile was sweet and she could see that Rick enjoyed it. Barbara licked her lips, which made her hot. "He read different books. Sometimes romance . . ."

Rick said, "Romance?"

Sarah cocked her head and frowned.

Rick cleared his throat. "Romance. Good for him." His expression was a mix of embarrassment and confusion. "Sorry, continue."

" . . . Romance, biology, mechanics, history."

Barbara interrupted, "History? As in ancient? World War II and things?"

Sarah shrugged. "Seemed to be recent. Some biography of past presidents. Some early 21st century stuff. He'd ask me odd questions."

Rick asked, "Such as?"

Sarah thought for a moment, "Like do I remember any significant events in the last ten years."

"Do you remember the first time he came in here?"

She bit her bottom lip. "Maybe five, six years ago. Maybe." She grinned. "I remember he looked lost and scared. Kind of like a two year old. It was so cute. He ordered a Baguette Pastrami and almost never changed . . ."

Rick and Barbara looked at one another.

Sarah continued, ". . . when I gave him the bill he handed me too much. I told him so, and he said, 'keep the change.' Bless his heart. He had been doing that ever since."

Rick leaned back and nodded. "Anything odd in the last year or two? Different behavior? Different company?"

Sarah suddenly said, "Yeah. About a year ago George started meeting some guy by the name of Alf or something like that. I couldn't tell the color of his hair. He wore an obvious wig, but to each his own. They talked politics, life, and lots of science. A few times they played chess. George almost always won. Then one day the guy stopped showing up."

"How long ago was that?" Rick asked.

Sarah thought. She sucked in one corner of her mouth for a few seconds. "Eight months ago, maybe more, maybe less. After that things seemed to be normal again. He'd either visit with Becky or by himself. Every now and then he'd talked to Joe."

Barbara asked, "Joe?"

Sarah nodded, "He's sitting there or had been." She pointed to where Joe had been sitting. It was at one of the corner booths.

Barbara spotted a man walking out the door in a hurry. He wore jeans, a brown t-shirt, and a Las Vegas Scarlet baseball cap.

Barbara nodded, leaned over toward Rick. "I'll handle this one."

Rick nodded.

Joe thought he had been pretty civil with Sarah. She'd talk to him but seemed never interested in him. Then that cop walked in yesterday. And she was sweet on him. He'd been trying for years to date her. Now that pissed him off. Time for another citizen to disappear he thought. Joe was halfway to his car when he heard someone yell his name. It was the Butch bitch who had been talking to Sarah. He stopped and turned toward her. "Yeah?"

Barbara flashed her badge. "I'd like to ask you a few question about George."

Joe thought 'fuck.' He considered running, but just as quickly decided against it. He'd play it cool and see how far this went. Worse case is that he could try and drop her, make a run for it, and head across the border for a few years. "Yes, ma'am?"

Barbara thought, 'Ma'am? Who was this guy kidding?' As she was within several feet she stopped and held out a picture of George. "Do you recognize this man?"

Joe nodded.

Barbara waited.

"That's George. He's been eatin' at the diner for years. What's up?"

Barbara smiled, "We're looking for him. You know where he is?"

Joe gave Barbara a deep frown. "Nope. The last time I saw him was sometime last week."

"Was he alone?"

Joe nodded.

Barbara waited.

"Yeah. He was alone. Reading a book, a pretty thick one."

"You ever talk to him?"

Joe held his breath, "We'd say hi to each other." He briefly looked away. "Sometimes talk about the weather."

Barbara nodded. She fished out a card from her pocket and handed it to Joe. "This has my contact info. If you see George, give me a call."

"Is he in trouble? I'm not feeling right about turning him in."

Barbara smiled, "It's something that could save his life."

Joe relaxed a bit. His smile was skewed. He nodded and gave Barbara another deep frown. "Alright, I'll do that."

Barbara backed up while Joe walked to his car, got in and sped off. She noted his license plate number. Once he was out of eyesight she called his plate in. A stream of data gave more insight to Joe than she expected. She walked back into the diner and found Rick and Sarah making light talk. Both sat in a booth.

Rick looked over to her and raised an eyebrow?

"He's a lying piece of work, but I got what I needed."

Sarah, surprised, said, "Joe? He's been coming here for years. He'd ask me out every now and then but he's always been nice and civil."

Barbara nodded. "Sarah, he's a predator . . ."

"What?"

". . . possibly a sociopath . . ."

"Order!" Mel shouted from the back.

"Keep that thought, "Sarah said as she walked through the kitchen doors.

Rick watched as she walked away into the kitchen. He gently sucked in his lower lip as he stared intently at her rear.

"Hey, Wolf!" Barbara said. "Was it good?"

"Barb!"

She smiled, "Well, partner? How was it?"

Rick kept his mouth shut, but his smile told everything.

"You are asking her out again tonight, yes?"

He frowned, "So soon?"

"I should kick you hard for that one."

Rick, confused, frowned.

"While the iron is hot, dude. While the iron is hot." She leaned back.

Rick coughed, "Besides the iron being hot, whatcha get from Joe?"

"He knew George personally. He tried to lie, but you know how that goes?"

"Closet boyfriend?"

Barbara shook her head. "Business. I've got a hunch that our Joe boy is not an upstanding citizen."

"Underground?"

Barbara nodded. "Yeah. Maybe the worst kind. And considering what really happened to George I got an idea who he may have last talked too."

"Seriously?"

Barbara nodded. "All of the above and then some."

Rick started, "We should . . ."

Sarah walked of the kitchen with plates in hand. "Now what were you saying about Joe?"

Barbara pouted fish lips and said, "Not the type of guy you want to be alone with. Probably rough and abusive, if you know what I mean."

"Really?" Her eyes quickly glanced over to Rick then back to Barbara.

"I chatted with him while you were in the kitchen. He said he may have said hi to George a few times."

Sarah frowned, shook her head slightly. "They've talked about a dozen times. Some pretty deep stuff from what I can tell."

Barbara said, "I thought as much. He's used to lying. Watch yourself around him."

Sarah nodded. "Tell me please, what is really going on?"

Rick said, "Sarah, nothing really. Following leads and Barb just happened upon someone to be leery about."

All three stood in silence for a moment.

Barbara kicked Rick.

"Stop kicking me, damn it."

Barbara leaned forward and whispered, "ask her."

"After talking about a sociopath?"

"Do it or I'll kick you again."

"Sarah," Rick began, "Free tonight?"

Sarah almost gushed. "Yeah, I am."

"How about a late dinner?"

She grinned and nodded.

"Steak dinner sound good?"

She nodded.

"Want me to pick you up here?"

She smiled again and handed him a piece of folded paper.

"Order!"

She blushed and rushed off.

Rick unfolded the paper. It was her address and personal iNum. He moved his leg out of the way just as Barbara's foot swung out. Her foot struck the foot backstop. With some deep perverse satisfaction Rick smiled. He looked Barbara in the eye and smiled.

She nodded approvingly.

***

Herb got up from the conference table and paced the floor. He stopped and looked at his team. Walt was going to write the Leads with Kimberly doing several technology and science pieces. Jaime would concentrate on scientist interviews. Vannessa and Ted would work Photography and archives. John and Heather worked copy. He scratched his left cheek and rubbed his chin. "Folks, this is big."

Everyone nodded.

"I know I keep mentioning it."

Several chuckled and everyone nodded.

Walt, slouching in his chair, said, "The Old Man. He's gotta know."

Herb paced again, "I know, I know." He stopped and sighed. "I know. I'll talk to Muhammad when he gets in. I gotta get him on board with this."

Jaime said, "Fuck. Really? The Gatekeeper has to be in on this?"

Herb replied, "He is my boss."

Walt said, "Sucks, but tell him, I'll go rogue if he blocks this one. Tell the Old Man that too. I ain't kidding. They bury this and they lose exclusivity."

Herb nodded. Walt would do it too. It wouldn't be the first time, so the threat had teeth.

Chapter 14

Becky said, "Are you sure you want to do this?'

Kent nodded. George had figured it out, but needed to slow the development of Transgenetics down. The drug was going to get FDA approval. It was going to become wildly popular. It was going to be a disaster. Humankind would fade away in less than a hundred years, or be heavily mutated with inbreeding, or worse. Kent suddenly got scared. The worst case scenario was not inbreeding. It was when humans had to artificially clone to produce kids. It would be a world of genetically manipulated test tube babies and artificial wombs.

"Which one first?" She asked.

***

Pete Walker woke up with a start. He wasn't supposed to be here. Not this place. Not this time. He reached up and felt the oxygen mask tightly over his mouth and nose. That was good, but he still wasn't supposed to be here. He couldn't. Damn! Another failure. And with that another chance at redemption. Maybe justice, too. All of which didn't matter at the moment. He had died, now he was awake. Pete took a deep breath and tested his eyes. The filtered light had a green tint to it, so the stinging shock of using his eyes for the first time wasn't so overly painful, just maybe annoying. Strands of long hair drifted in front of his eyes. Strange he thought. 'My hair grew longer while asleep?' He made a mental note to check the software and chamber. He hoped he was the first to waken. Any technical glitches he could correct. He took another deep breath and tested his hands. Each finger flexed. That was good, but they looked smaller than he remembered. Was it the effect of the stasis goo, or was there something seriously wrong with the cloning process? He looked up at a blinking display board over his head. It flashed "Purge in progress. Please standby." He looked around and spotted the readout displays to his right. Little monitors flashed and displayed numbers and text. One display was counting down. Another was scrolling odd bits of information, like "You can do it!", "This time for sure!", "So close, yet so far!", "It's time to leave. Prepare." That he thought odd. He looked over at the monitor that was displaying a countdown of sorts. Then he remembered. "Purge in progress." He looked up and saw two metal rings. He grabbed them. Seconds later he felt the floor underneath his feet vanish. The green tinted fluid slipped away from his eyesight. He remembered the process now. He waited until the fluid completely drained. The system would cycle through several procedures. Purge was first, wash was second. Release was third. He counted to three and the floor came back. Seconds later the container he was in filled with some clear fluid – water he thought. It was warm and turbulent, like a washing machine. Minutes ticked by as the chamber filled, circulated, and drained several times. The little countdown display kept track and reminded him he was not the original. Intellectually he understood he was not the original. Waking up in a thick green goo fluid reinforced that, too. When the countdown display reached zero he was hit with a blast of hot air. It whirled around him rapidly. He was dry in seconds. He lowered himself far enough to feel the grid floor and tested his legs. Strong, firm, stable. He let go of the overhead rings and with his weight fully supported by his feet he unsnapped his harness. There was something he was supposed to remember. Then he looked up and saw faces staring back at him. 'WTF,' was his first thought. 'How?', was the second thought. Moments later the door disappeared and a hand offered to help him out. He was weak and gladly accepted the familiar looking hand. Once passed the chamber threshold he took off the mask.

Kent helped Pete out of the chamber. Even after waking the others it was still amazing and un-nerving in watching the entire process. It was even more startling to see himself as a woman – not once, but four times. This Pete was the last one he was going to wake up. The big guy was going to sleep forever – if he could help it. The thought of this massive brute awake and causing havoc was unthinkable. "Welcome to your day one, Pete."

Pete looked around, blinked several times, looked down and noticed firm breasts, inhaled deeply, then fainted.

Kent caught her. The first female Pete laughed first, then fainted. That gave him time to catch her. The second female Pete smiled, felt her breast, reached between her legs, found nothing, fainted. The third female Pete cursed up a blue streak. She stayed angry for hours.

***

Everyone in the auditorium sat in the large upholstered chairs. Kent walked up to the front and took a deep breath. This was George's plan, but he agreed. George worked out the details. "I am truly sorry we are here." He surveyed the many different faces. Some sad, some angry, some stoic. It was amazing the different range of emotions he saw. They were essentially the same person, and so they should, at least, show the same expression given all were in the same situation. That's what he thought, but standing in front of all the different incarnations of Pete Walker showed otherwise. Each person seemed to truly be unique.

Prax had finished passing out the last sandwiches and adult beverage. Even the two physically looking teenagers had wine. Technically they were all newborns, but no one objected to the Sangria sitting in front of them.

"There are three options you have. Accept who you are, why you are here, and work with me. If we succeed we may all live normal lives. That's option one. The other options are to be angry and stay angry. Hate everything and everyone. Make life suck for yourself. I would say you can either go back into the stasis chamber, drift until whenever, or have Mike fix your last meal."

Silence.

The phrase 'talking to oneself' had special meaning here. He waited a moment. No one objected. "Right after I woke up, I discovered George – Pete five, had blown himself up in an attempt to slow down Forever Life and its soon to be released drug called Transgenetics. I wrestled for days wondering why he would do such a thing. He killed about 30 individuals and injured over a hundred. George had prerecorded information. He had physical items he collected during his six years living . . ." Kent heard several gasps. He was getting their attention. "I also have about a years' worth of his memory."

Someone raised a hand and said, "How long?"

"We've been in stasis for twenty some-odd years. The world is better and worse at the same time. Social classes are still divided but by greater numbers, the top 1% own about eight-five percent of the US wealth. The Dow hit 25,000 yesterday – and that is not even the record. We are strangers in a strange land. There's been a brief nuclear war – Iran turned mostly to glass, Russia in financial ruin, China had a major depression. The US became independent from foreign oil 13 years ago and became a major exporter of natural gas and petro. Fifty percent of the country is powered by renewable energy."

Another voice asked, "How old are you?"

"Seven days."

"Who's the female?"

"Our lighthouse in dark times."

Everyone stood up and turned to Becky.

The motion startled her. Different faces intensely

staring, but seemingly of the same mind and body – potential George like. She shivered.

Kent said, "She's been with us for six years. George trusted her one hundred percent. So do I. Absolutely, with no reservations."

"How?" A male voice shouted out.

"Even before I transferred George's memories I trusted her. I trust Mike and I trust Prax." Actually, he mostly trusted Mike and Prax, but he wasn't going to voice that. Not here inside the complex.

Everyone sat down. It was eerie.

The African-American version of Pete stood up. He looked around. "This is creeping me out, but Pete Prime had a plan. Sucks big time that we are here. I remember why I was created, and I feel a need to act on that reason. But something is wrong. It's like we've gone off program?" He sat down.

Kent nodded. "I felt the same way, but George told . . ."

A female version stood up, "Excuse me, sorry. But 'George'?"

Kent took a deep breath. "It was Kevin, Pete Four, who re-established the tradition of choosing a name. I am Kent. Pete One took the name Eugene, but Pete two and three did not take a name. Kevin said it took him years to come to grips that he was not Pete Prime. George, Pete Five, said it took him months. It took me a day. George said that we are individuals and therefore should live not in Pete's shadow, but create our own path, he . . ."

The female, still standing, interrupted, "So, basically, I can walk out of here?"

All heads turned to her.

Kent nodded, "Yes, you can. I won't stop you. Mike, would you stop her?"

Mike's voice filled the room, "No, Kent. Pete Eight may leave anytime, though I suggest she wait until I can establish a plausible background accompanied by the necessary paperwork and identification. It would also be prudent for Pete Eight, or anyone else, to study the last twenty years of changes. The world is different enough to warrant a sensible sound judgment in getting to know it first."

She sat down.

Kent counted to ten before continuing. "He said the sooner you pick a name the better."

"Can we view this video?"

"Mike?"

"Yes, Kent?"

"Please play the first video I viewed."

The room darkened.

The center display screen came to life. His face appeared with a relaxed smile. "Mike," George said over his shoulder, "I'm ready."

"Yes Doctor Walker. Recording now."

George cleared his voice. "Number six, sorry I couldn't welcome you into the world personally. I should have started recording a daily log day one, but . . ." He shrugged. "You'll discover things tend to get lost in translating and we Walkers tend to become self-absorbed." His smile was still alarming. "Remember that, okay. First, change your first name. I am not Pete. Neither are you. We are our own individuals." The image leaned forward. "Yes we share memories with Pete, but we are not him. The moment you opened your eyes you became your own person." He leaned back. "Remember me as George. Keep the family name but lose the first. Seriously. It took me several months to understand that. Kevin, number four, told me to change my name. I fought it. Just fought it. Then one day I realized Pete and I had nothing substantive in common. I read romance, he read non-fiction. I like Pistachio ice cream. He was a vanilla man. You getting the picture yet?"

Kent looked over his brethren. They all remained fixated on the main screen.

"About Mike. Don't ask if he is a real person. Mike will give you the silent treatment for days. If you did ask apologize, now. Seriously. Apologize. You'll need his help."

Kent remembered and smiled.

"Number six, I'd like to tell you to forget our quest. You know, live your own life. Start a family. Have two and one-half kids running around. . ." George suddenly looked ten years older. "Forrest Taylor has to be stopped. Brother six, Forrest has to be stopped." He leaned back and looked sad. "I've been fighting this bastard for six years now. I've been able to uncover a lot as were the others: Kevin, Pete 3, Pete 2, and Eugene. Forrest's plan is worse than anyone can imagine. Sick bastard." Suddenly George stood up and walked away. "Mike, pause recording please. Thanks." The image of a receding George froze in mid step.

Kent said, "Resume please, Mike. Thanks."

The video resumed and George gave them a rundown on major milestones in US and World Politics and History. The room's vibe shifted when George talked about number eighteen. " . . . He'll have one thought.

Destroy. If he wakes up, then Forrest succeeded and all of humankind, at least in nations where the wealthy can afford the drugs, he'll have one preprogrammed thought. Soon after he wakes he'll double in size. He'll get no last message because he won't understand. Mike will send him immediately to the surface. No help, no prep, nothing. Because it won't matter. He'll destroy. He'll run the distance from here to the Taylor Building and destroy. Everything. Everything. He's not number eighteen, he's Omega." George looked up at some part of the room. "Everything." He rubbed his chin. "Enough of doomageddon . . ."

Becky watched with a heavy heart. This was a recording she had never seen. Her George, gone.

The lights turned on. The auditorium was silent for a moment.

Kent stood up. "Of course, you can go through any and all the other recordings. You may even take George's memories, but I have to warn you. It contains emotions." He looked toward Becky and smiled.

She blushed.

"And the emotions are very powerful, and very real."

Everyone turned to Becky.

Her blush darkened and she looked down with teary eyes. She acted like she hadn't noticed.

Kent said, "There's another video I should show. Mike, please show the one were George reveals who Forrest is."

"Of course, Kent."

The monitor lit up with George sitting at the desk. His hair was messy and he had a five-day old beard. His eyes were bloodshot with hooded eyelids. "This is madness. It's been two weeks and I haven't slept well. Kevin, that's the name number four chose, said that Forrest's company Forever Life submitted an investigational New Drug application to CDER. Apparently, he was going to sabotage the application, but didn't succeed. I woke up two weeks ago and binged on all the information about Forrest and Forever Life, Inc. This is crazy. Forrest is our Alpha! He was the first successful clone and we are working against him!" The screen went black for a few seconds. A new image appeared. "Forrest is out of his mind. He has to be. I see why, Pete Prime broke ties with him and made this place. Transgenetics can transform the entire world to something good. Think about it. A pill that acts as a transport and vector for radical morphologic change, but Forrest has a secret agenda. He wants to make the world shaped in his image." The screen went black a few seconds, then George reappeared. "I've been alive for about six months now. This world is amazing! Cars that drive themselves? Androids? Of which I'm going to have to make one. Space travel? Vacations in Earth's orbit. Opportunities? Endless." The screen went black and the lights came on.

Kent said, "There are other videos I hadn't seen yet. Mostly are of George making self-notes. He talks about what he discovered during one of those sleepless weeks."

One of the Pete teenagers said, "What are you not telling us?"

Kent gave out a light laugh. "Is it that obvious?"

The other teenager coughed, "Hello, clone here. We all have the same thoughts."

The others gave out a nervous laugh.

Kent nodded, "That part may surprise you?"

Someone else said, "Pardon?"

Kent took a deep breathe. "We are related to Pete, not his exact clone."

Everyone, said, "Wait, what?" There was a pause then the entire auditorium erupted into laughter.

Kent relaxed. He nodded. "The only true way to go beyond the seven clone limit is to keep using original adult stem cells for the donor. Young cells. The cells cannot come from a donor in advanced age. Between 25 and 35 for females and 18 to 25 for males seems to be the best. So, there is a time limit. Clone young and often or clone old and done. That's why Pete Prime used other genetic donors. That's why we are here."

One of the females stood up, "But, female?!?"

"Or a midget!" A voice said from one of the seats.

"Or Black?!?"

"Or Asian?!?"

Kent said, "Pete Prime had his reasons. He left no videos."

Mike interjected, "Kent, please excuse my intrusion. Pete Prime did leave an audio message."

"I apologize to those listening. I am sorry to have brought you into this world. I am dead. Maybe a few years, maybe a hundred now, but I am dead and have no way to make up for bringing you to life. But it was necessary. You see, the whole of humankind is in danger. Dichotomously you are here. My sacrifice to help the world and my selfishness for creating you. So, why did I create you? Clones Beta to Eta should be obvious. Revenge mostly, but to continue where I left off. In making Beta to Eta I gambled that I would have to try all the obvious means to stop Forrest, which you know to be Alpha. In the beginning we created Forever Life and Transgenetics to help humankind. We both shared a dream that one day all cancer, illnesses, deformities, psychoses, any and everything that caused suffering in humankind could and would be a thing of the past. It really was a good dream, but Forrest, at some point changed. My fault maybe . . . no . . . my fault period. I brought him into the world thinking that we were of one mind – mine. How naïve. One cannot create life and hope to micromanage that life into an aligned belief . . ." He sighed. "Forrest became his own person and we had a difference of opinion. Maybe I was wrong in creating you, but . . ." There was a long pause. "Forgive me, please." His voice cracked. "I just wanted to make the world a better place. Now I want to fix this, but I know I may not see the end and that hurts. So, please understand I'm not holding you to correct the problem I made. If you are listening to this I am gone, but this is your world now. You have no choice except, work to fix it, live with it, or take the easy way out by suicide. I certainly can't pass judgment." Another long pause. "One last thing. As you may or may not know, we are related. We are not identical. You have your own soul and dharma to live with. There's no test known to humankind that would prove you to be clones. Think about that. No test, period."

Mike said, "That is all. Pete Prime never made video recordings."

Kent said, "Is Pete correct about no test could prove we are clones?"

"None."

Kent nodded as did everyone in the room. They remained silent for a moment. Kent said, "Questions?"

Pete Midget stood on the chair. "I might be the most disadvantaged here. What is the world like for little people?"

Becky walked close to Kent. "I can answer that." All heads turned toward her. She took a deep breath and let it out slowly. "You'd find it surprisingly well and accommodating. The LPA is a very powerful organization and lobbying group. There are about 23 representatives in Congress and three in the Senate. Two governors and over 50 mayors are LPs. Buildings built after 2025 have door knobs lowered by six inches. ATM have a secondary access keypad and screen. Elevator buttons lowered. Restaurant chairs and booths have built in steps and adjustable seats. Cars come standard with steering wheel brakes and accelerators. Google's autonomous cars are very popular with the LP community.

"Excuse me? LP?"

Becky nodded. "Little People. The term Dwarf and Midget fell out of favor before 2010. Short-statured is commonly used, though sometimes in a derogatory way with the right fringe, but they'll never change. They hate everyone not white, Christian, and who believe the Earth is greater than 6,000 years old."

"Thank you." Pete LP sat down.

Pete African-American stood up. "And blacks?"

Becky smiled, "Two black presidents. Two added to the Supreme Court. The third richest man in America is black. We're talking billionaire. Hundreds into the billion. Public figures have been caught lying about having black ancestors. Very embarrassing. And a third of the richest most powerful fortune 500 companies have black CEOs." She stepped closer to Kent. "And for women, the ERA passed."

Kent said, "Mike?"

"Yes, Kent?"

"I vaguely remember a conference room. Do we still have one?"

"We do. Ms. Becky knows the way."

Kent, embarrassed, said, "Sorry. The memories say you know the place better than George did, but my mind is still trying to grasp that fact. Sorry." He looked down.

Becky grabbed his hand and smiled. "Follow me."

He looked up teary eyed and grabbed her out stretched hand.

She led him out the door of the main auditorium, down one of several hallways, into a large room with a large table. Thirteen chairs. Large screen display monitors hung on three of the walls.

The others followed and took their seats. Groups started forming. The females sat together, the short-statured Pete sat next to the teenagers.

Kent stood at the head of the table. "Mike, could you please display, in tile format, an image of each Pete with space enough for a name?"

All three monitors flashed on with snapshots of each clone blocked out across each screen in three rows.

LP Pete said, "I kind of want to get some thoughts out in the air. I'm sure I'm not the only one thinking some rather progressive, if not perverted thoughts."

Several in the room coughed.

Kent nodded. "I, too, had been thinking that, but didn't want to bring it up just yet."

Strawberry blond Pete laughed nervously, "We are

thinking alike." She reached under her shirt and started playing with a breast. "Goddamn this feels good!"

Everyone laughed and the tension in the room evaporated.

Asian Pete exclaimed, "Bastard had an ego!" He grabbed himself, "Do all the guys have big dicks now?"

LP Pete stood up on the table, holding himself, and said out loud, "Ha! I'm tripod man!"

More laughter.

In all the years Mike observed the Petes he had never once turned off his cameras. Today was an exception. Five hours' worth of exception.

Chapter 15

Thompson sat at his desk reviewing a new case. There was another bombing, but this time no one was hurt. The Division suspected a local militia – The Libertarians for Independent American Rule and Security. Barbara had a possible lead, but he dropped off the radar. Thompson was about to open a FaceRec file when there was a knock at the door. He looked up, "Yes?"

One of the Desk Sergeants was holding a small delivery box. "Thompson, something for you."

Thompson got up and took the box from the Sergeant's outstretched arm. "Feels fairly heavy."

The Sergeant nodded. "DeepScan gives it an okay, but we have the carrier in hold until you check it out."

Thompson nodded and sat down at his desk. He pulled on the release tape and the box opened. "Wow!"

"Something interesting?"

Thompson drew out a long whistle. "I'll say. This is a pretty big SolidState. Maybe a Quad of storage. Either this is overkill or I'm gonna be here for a while. Let the carrier cool off for several hours."

"Pretty long time."

Thompson turned the empty box over several

times. No return tag, QrCode, or bar address. Not even a printed InDent."

The Sergeant nodded again. "Yeah, the main reason he's waiting."

"How long can you hold . . . him?"

The Sergeant nodded.

". . . hold him?"

"Two hours tops."

"Okay thanks. It'll be an hour to dup the thing. I can't image someone sending such an expensive hardware for a couple of pics." He sucked in his lips. "Two hours then."

The Sergeant closed the door on the way out as Thompson pressed the InterCom button on his console. "Team, we got a mystery. A new game is afoot. Allonsy!"

***

Forrest read the report. A second time. Someone hacked the system last night. Luckily, nothing of value was stolen, but it was annoying. Forever Life's closest competitor tried regularly to hack the system and regularly failed. Once they managed to breach the firewall. They found a backdoor through a new employee – he was fired of course, but the damage had been done. They had been in the system for a week before security spotted, quarantined, and deleted the plant. But this time was different. This hack, it was discovered, had inside help from a plant that had been in the system, from what the report said, for years. It lay dormant all this time - through numerous updates and upgrades, until it needed to open a doorway for the hack. Forrest turned and faced the window. A reflection of himself showed a man frowning deeply. He thought it had to have been the work of Pete. Who else would have this kind of patience? He tapped at the 'Intercom' icon on his desk. "Troy. Step into my office please."

A moment later Troy entered. He walked the long distance from the front door to Forrest's desk. "Yes, sir?"

"Have a seat, please."

Troy swallowed hard. Mr. Taylor never invited him to sit. "Is everything okay, sir?" He said while sitting.

Forrest smiled. He liked Troy. Of all his assistants Troy was the most capable. Beyond his wildest dreams. The man, who could easily have started his own company and succeeded well, had several degrees. He composed himself well as he faced Forrest. Troy knew a lot of his secrets but not the uber ones. "How are you with a gun?"

Troy slowly took a breath. Is Mr. Taylor going to ask him to do some wet work? Oh, Most High Goddess he thought. "I'm good. I have Master shooter status with a 10 mil short nose."

Forrest nodded and smiled. "Good. How would you like to get out into the field more often?"

"Sir. You may ask anything . . ."

Forrest tilted his head back. "Anything?" His smile widened. "You're not completing the sentence tells me there is a line."

Troy slowly nodded. He swallowed hard.

Forrest laughed and Troy nervously joined him. A moment later Forrest cleared his throat. "How are your fighting skills?" He knew the answer, of course.

He knew everything about the man. Including past, present, and possibly future lovers.

"Aikido, sir. Instructor level."

"Have you ever maimed anyone?"

"Never, but I'd never been given an opportunity."

"What about killing?"

He hesitated a split second. "In self-defense, I can live with that."

Forrest pressed, "And offensively?"

Silence hung in the air awkwardly.

Forrest repeated the question. "And offensively?"

Troy cleared his throat. "I don't know."

Forrest raised an eyebrow. "Really? You've never thought about it?"

"I've thought about it, yes. But to actively . . ."

Forrest leaned back in his chair. "And?"

Troy took a deep breathe. Was he being interviewed? Near terror gripped his heart, but he managed to not show his distress. At least he hoped it didn't show.

Forrest waited. He could see the turmoil splashed across the man's face.

Troy finally said, "I would have a problem with that, but I'd get over it. Eventually."

Forrest nodded, but didn't smile.

Troy noticed and added. "There are incentives to help accept things that are unpleasant . . . sir, am I being interviewed for a position change?"

Forrest smiled. "Yes. How do you feel about that?"

"The fact that we are talking flatters me." He cleared his throated but immediately wished he hadn't. "I'd like to think that you value my service."

"I do, hence here we are."

Troy nodded.

"Would you like to know the position?"

Troy nodded, and suddenly it dawned on him. "Bodyguard."

Forrest nearly laughed. "Very good! I'll be venturing out into the public soon . . . ," he shrugged, ". . . and I'll need someone with a cool head to watch my back – so to speak."

Troy frowned. "Why not a SU?"

"I'll need a human handler. Our Security Units are the best money can buy, but . . . I need a human supervisor to judge, ultimately, when not to shoot."

Troy thought about that. "I understand, sir. Will this be full-time?"

Forrest nodded. "For the moment, you'll continue your duties as my assistant. When I need to venture outside off the radar you will accompany me. I'll let you select your replacement when time comes for you to be fully engaged in your new position."

Troy nodded.

"Think of it as an extension of what you do now, but with added benefits, perks, and pay."

"I understand, sir. When do I start?"

"Now. I won't be touring the city yet, but that shouldn't stop you from getting a Mark 10. Draft up the necessary paperwork and I'll sign it."

Troy nodded. "Thank you, sir."

"What are you doing tonight?"

Troy pursed his lips shook his head, "Nothing, sir."

"Good." He held out a business card.

Troy took the card and looked at it. It read 'Bechard & Hernandez Security Tactical Group'.

"Ms. Bechard will be sending someone this afternoon to see you. Your training starts tonight."

Troy nodded, picked up the signal that the meeting was over, got up. "Very good, sir."

Forrest watched Troy walk the length from his desk to the door. Seconds later, he was alone again. He reached into a small drawer located on the inside of his desk. He hadn't used the mobile phone for over a year, but the battery indicator showed 100% charged. He took a deep breath and pressed the call button. Only one phone would ring. George gave it to him three years ago. He had wanted to destroy the thing, but nostalgia and a lack of true friends kept him from doing so. The last time he and George parted hadn't been on the best of terms. They negotiated for months, exchanged data, findings, notes, then . . . a disagreement. He wanted the last couple of steps to cloning. George wanted the last datum on Transgenetics. Neither of them would budge. They both parted in the worst of terms. A stinging bitter taste that lingered for months. In the end, George stepped up his espionage, of which cost him a life. He had his top tech geeks try and trace the signals, but it was nearly impossible. There had been 25 hops to a supposedly dead cell tower. Ironically, it was located across the street from the Forever Life building. Tracing the wired path proved fruitless as there had been no less than thirty repeaters and over a dozen cross-connects across the city. Cutting off one connection took down an entire block. Unexpectedly the ringing stopped. A robotic male voice said, "Forrest. It's been a long time. Hold please." Forrest recognized it to be Mike's.

Forrest subconsciously answered, "Of course, thank you." He felt a rush of emotion. Raw, intense stream of loss. He considered George more a friend than an adversary, but such was the way of business. One clamped down on weak feelings and embraced the emotions and thoughts that allowed one to succeed. 'Was that the way it really should be?'

Kent thought it interesting that Pete used a dining table for the conference room. It was an extra-large Stickley Highlands Double Pedestal dining table. The dark brown oak top was scratched heavily, but Pete decided to never make any repairs. He had it sneaked in, through one of the many special entry ways, under the cloak of darkness some years ago. One of the more noticeable scratches was caused by the move. Now Kent found himself strangely fixated on the table's top. He looked up and noticed everyone else except Becky staring at the same spot – the one made during the clandestine move. The others looked up too and the room filled with a slow buildup of nervous laughter.

LP Pete said, "Seriously, this is kind of creepy."

Strawberry Pete nodded, "Are we going to do this forever?"

Tall Pete spoke for the first time, "Probably so." He chuckled. "And the reactions we'll get."

Black Pete said, "What am I thinking?"

Without hesitation half the group said, "Rumpelstiltskin." While a fourth said, "Let down your hair." The rest said, "Maleficient."

Kent said, "Do or do not."

Black Pete, "Rumpelstiltskin has it, but I did think 'Let down your hair,' first and had a flash of Angelina in Maleficient."

LP Pete said, "Still creepy, but interesting. Are we starting to think differently from one another?"

Strawberry Pete said, "Kent. You said, 'Do or do not.' Episode five. I can't say I wasn't thinking Star Wars, especially the Clone Wars, which is ironic by itself. Is it because you've been out the longest that you are thinking differently?"

Kent shrugged and said, "I wouldn't say I'm thinking differently, just maybe on a different thought track. But it's looking like divergent thought is beginning. And that is a good thing."

"Explain, please." Asian Pete asked.

"The fact that you're asking that question means you are diverging."

Asian Pete looked around. "Who else thought that question?"

Tall Pete raised a hand. So did Pete seven and Teenage Male Pete.

"I understand the process," Teenage Male Pete started, "but am I comfortable about it?" He shrugged. "It's only been a day and I'm afraid I'm gonna lose everyone here."

Everyone in the room nodded.

Kent said, "Can anyone guess what I'm thinking?"

The two teenaged Petes stood, looked at one another and laughed for a moment. In unison they said, "Can we read each other's minds?"

Kent smiled, "Creepy is a good word." He pointed to Tall Pete.

Tall Pete said, "What . . ."

Strawberry Pete said, ". . . am . . ."

LP Pete said, ". . . I . . ."

Black Pete said, ". . . doing . . ."

Nervous laughter spread through the room.

Pete eight said, ". . . here?"

Then silence.

Prax entered the room. He held a mobile phone in a hand and walked toward Kent. When he was within reach he stopped and held the phone out to Kent.

Kent swallowed hard. This was it. This was the answer to, 'What am I doing here.' He looked around the room. All earnest faces on him now. He took the phone and put it on speaker. Clearing his throat he said, "Pete six, speaking. Brother Forrest, we never met."

Forrest's voice projected out past the tiny speakers. "Hello, Pete."

Kent clicked the volume to its loudest and said, "Six, please."

"Pardon?"

"Pete Six. I'm Pete Six."

"Forgive me, Pete Six. All is well I hope?"

Absently Kent nodded, "Quite. I'm very comfortable these days, though not quite in the lap of luxury you're accustomed too."

There was an audible sigh. "Pete Six, I'd like to call a truce."

Kent lifted an index finger to his lips. "One calls a truce when one worries the tides of war are not turning from one's shores."

There was a long pause.

"You have George's memory."

Kent smiled. "I have enough, Forrest. I have enough."

Another long pause.

"I'd like to discuss our future."

"Our's? As in, you and me? My future is looking very nice."

"Is there a Pete Seven?"

"Waiting to be woken up? Ha! I can honestly say I

am truly the last of the Pete Walkers, Alpha."

"Then you see a future of non-violence?"

"I see a future with a world not on a path to incest or sterilization."

"Our figures tell us otherwise and . . ."

Kent exploded, "Are wrong!"

"We've gone over this!"

Kent laughed. "You and George have. I re-ran his figures and completely agree with him. You're gonna doom an entire generation of most of the world for money."

"Pete Six, please, this is not how I wanted to rekindle contact with family. I just want to talk."

"Talk then."

A pretty loud sigh. "Not over this thing. Face to face."

Kent remained silent for a moment. He yawned and looked at his nails.

"Are you still there?"

"I am."

"And?"

"And, back."

"Damn you. Please."

Kent smiled. "The Lo'tion."

"Tomorrow?"

"Day after. I have something to do tomorrow."

"Day after then. Lunch?"

"Yeah, after one would be nice. You pay. One bodyguard, no Security Units. . ."

"Not acceptable . . ."

"I hope your bodyguard is sweet to look at or can hold a conversation."

"A bodyguard then."

"One human."

"A human and one android."

"That'll be a table for three then. Your android eat meat?"

After a pause, "Okay. One human bodyguard. But I must have a Security team nearby. You got to grant me that. Please."

"There's a shopping mall about five blocks away. One vehicle, park them there."

"Agreed."

"I'll know if you have more than one and if they are not there . . ."

"How would you possibl . . ."

"Alpha, stop. My terms or you enjoy eating lunch with your bodyguard."

Kent ended the call before Forrest could say anything else. Only then did he allow himself a moment to exhale. He looked around the room. All eyes were on him.

LP Pete said, "Fuck," and laughed.

The others joined in. Kent blushed.

Forrest nearly threw the phone across the room. 'The arrogant fuck,' he thought. He totally dominated the conversation, controlled the conditions, and dictated the terms. He was better than George and that worried him. 'I can honestly say I am truly the last of the Pete Walkers, Alpha.' Odd. 'Last of the Pete Walkers'. Forrest placed the phone back in its secret spot. He pressed the intercom icon on his desk. "Troy?"

"Yes, sir?"

"Has Ms. Bechard's rep contacted you?"

"Yes, sir. I'll be visiting their training facility at seven."

"Very good. Take the rest of the day off then. I'm going home."

"Is everything alright, sir?"

"Well enough, but . . ." He let the sentence linger.

"Understood. Personal mode or autonomous?"

"Autonomous please."

"Unit three will meet you in the garage, sir."

Subconsciously Forrest nodded, "Very good." He clicked off.

'I can honestly say I am truly the last of the Pete Walkers, Alpha.' Forrest thought, 'that is a message to me, but what does it mean?'

Chapter 16

"Pearl. I want to be known as Pearl." Strawberry Blond Pete said.

The image of Strawberry Blond Pete displayed 'Pearl' as the caption.

Kent asked, "Anyone else?"

Pete Seven said, "Call me Megan." Her new name appeared under her picture.

LP Pete cleared his throat. "Marty for me."

"Morgan. Call me Morgan." Black Pete said.

"Jackie," Asian Pete said.

Everyone in the room turned and looked at Jackie.

Barbara said, "What's wrong with Jackie?"

Everyone laughed.

Kent said, "Umm, dude. As in Jackie Chan?"

Jackie smiled and shrugged. "Jet would have been too obvious and Bruce . . ."

Tall Pete yelled, ". . . is my choice."

Jackie continued, "Which is better than Morgan Freeman!"

Morgan replied, "Or Marty McFly!"

More laughter.

New names appeared under each picture until only two Petes, the teenagers, were left?

Both looked up. They had been whispering between the two. Teenager Male looked at Teenager Female. "Me, or you?"

Teenager Female said, "Sequenced."

He nodded, took a deep breath, and said in German accented English, "Hi, my name is Hans."

"And, I'm Gretel." She said in an equally bad German accent.

Kent face palmed himself while everyone laughed.

Marty turned to Kent, "So Father . . ."

Kent interrupted, "of which I'm not sure I like."

Pearl said, "No choice, Father."

Kent groaned.

Gretel spoke up, "Okay, we'll only call you Father in private . . ."

"Except for Gretel and myself, "Hans said. "We can get away with it."

"Okay, okay, okay." Kent gave in. Then he laughed. It was slow at first. One hardly realized he had been laughing, then it crescendo rather quickly.

Becky cocked her head. "What's so funny?"

Kent took a deep breath and relaxed. His eyes watered as he smiled.

Becky asked, "And?"

He looked up and over to Pearl.

She smiled and said, "Mother."

Becky smiled, "I'm a lot younger than you think."

"Oh?" Kent said. He scrunched his face up and thought hard. "Becky, I don't know how old you are. Now that is odd. Didn't George know?"

She answered, her grin turned sly, "I needed to keep some secrets."

Brunette Pete, now named Carrie, said, "Guys, guys.

The plan?"

Kent nodded. "George had worked out a plan years ago, but he only wanted to do it as a last resort. In a way, he didn't want to wake you guys up. He . . ."

"Why?" Jackie said.

"Do I really have to explain?"

Jackie thought about it. "I suppose not. We are not what we expected to be. I'm warming up to the idea of not being Middle Asian . . . I guess." He frowned. "No, I'm not warming up to the idea. As a matter of fact, I'm mad as hell. Pete fucked us in one way or another. This face I see in the mirror is not me."

Morgan nodded, "I agree. I think we all agree. How in the hell am I supposed to act?" He suddenly looked exasperated. "I'm black. And I have a whole lot of baggage I'm not ready to deal with."

Pearl said, "Deal with? Not ready? At least you are still male." She stood up. "What about us?" She gestured toward the three women next to her and over to Gretel. "You want a life event change? Wake up a girl." She sat down.

Gretel said, "Wake up a girl in her teens. What do we know about being female? You guys can fake it pretty easy. When I last went to the restroom I stood frozen for several minutes wondering how am I going to pee? Sit down you say? I got too many programmed years of standing up. How long will it take for me to realize standing up in a restroom is not an easy option? How long will it take for me to automatically wipe away instead of toward? And, dear God, what happens when I have a period? Cry me a river, huh? I'm with George. I got no choice, but damn, this day-dream is really a nightmare with the lights on."

The room fell silent.

Kent nodded, sighed, and said, "I got a chuck of George's memories. That part is strong. He really thought Pete Prime was a mothafucker for doing this. I agree. And, I have to say I am fortunate. I am still white. But I also had to learn that white is no longer an advantage in the World. In 2031 whites became a minority in America. And what a slap to the face that had been. One day we're a top, the next we're a reluctant forced bottom. White was no longer right. That was about several years of cold water in the face wake up. So, I got my own adjustments to do. Not nearly as rough as everyone else, of course, in this room, but I do get it. And, that's the bleed out. But we do have the option to settle the score with the big picture now . . ." He stabbed his right-hand index finger toward the ground, "and later we can deal with the personal traumas."

Bruce asked, "Father, we hear you . . . I hear you. What do we do?"

Kent looked around the room. Sullen and determined faces looked back. "After we do this, success or failure, we walk away."

"Really?"

He nodded. "Absolutely really. This is the last stand, but it doesn't have to be in a blaze of muzzle flashes. We do it and we move on. How many of you want to spend a short life fighting a behemoth?"

No one said anything.

"I don't want to die. And, I think that comes from the fact that they'll never be another Pete look-alike again. You guys are proof of that. George saved his memory. He knew I would awaken and would source his memory. He knew there was another him coming. I don't have that luxury. Everyone that matters is awake now."

"The Big guy?" Marty offered.

Kent replied, "Is Doo-Ma-Uck-Up-Ge-Don." He shook his head. "He scares me and that's the option I don't think I ever want to pick."

"We can't picket Alpha's building . . . wait. Do they even picket these days?"

Becky said, "It's still allowed, but you need a special permit."

Marty continued, "We can't picket Alpha's building with signs saying evil monster."

Kent replied, "We can but we can do something better."

"Like what?" Morgan asked.

Kent smiled. "Think about it. We all have the same base gene."

The room remained quiet for a moment.

Pearl laughed out loud.

Kent said, "That's one. Who else?"

Marty looked around the room. All his brothers and sisters were in deep thought. Kent said, '. . . same base gene'. Marty repeated the phrase a dozen times in his head. They were all related . . . but the world didn't know that. How could they? He smiled and laughed out loud.

Bruce noted that half his brothers and sisters laughed and giggled. How easily they figured it out . . . maybe? He knew what Transgenetics did. So, what was the connection? Same gene base meant related, yet how would the world know they were related by a common gene? We have the same last name . .

. ha! The world doesn't know that he thought. Early experiments and unofficial trials? That would be unethical! He looked Kent in the eye. Kent smiled and nodded. Silently he mouthed, "You figured it out?" Bruce nodded and gave the biggest smile he could muster. The world would see Forever Life as unethical, careless, and callous. Profit and greed above public safety interest. Unsanctioned early human trials. How many laws would that have broken? Maybe the uckin' bastard Pete Prime had figured it out early or he was one goddam lucky sumbitch. Brilliant!

Kent said, "Transgenetics is entering human trials. George figured we can expose TransG as evil just by presenting ourselves as early clandestine drug recipients." He let that linger in the air.

Marty stood up, "Wait, what? We expose ourselves? Are you saying . . . wait . . . I get it. DNA testing could show that our DNA had been "altered" to a common DNA and . . ."

Jackie stood up, ". . . exposes humans to eventual inbreeding . . ."

Megan said, ". . . in the very near future."

The group spontaneously started laughing.

Becky cringed. They all had the same type of laugh. Every one of them. Uck! No, that was double uck and then some.

Chapter 17

Rick and Barbara walked into the Lo'tion. It was unusually crowded for this time of day. Sarah greeted Rick with a warm smile. She walked over and brushed her hand over his.

He smiled, "Hey Sarah. You look nice."

She blushed. "Thanks."

Barbara puffed her cheeks out as if about to throw up. "Love birds. Ah yes, I remember the moment. Pleasant. Hey Sarah, I'm hungry." She looked around. "Got a table for us? This place is crowded. You guys ran some ad on the local stream?"

Sarah shook her head, "No, but man has it been busy. Nearly everyone here is trying a Pastrami on Baguette."

Barbara said, "Seriously? Is it really that good?"

Sarah nodded, "It is. Mel's outdone himself. He uses the best baguettes, which we are fast running out of, fresh romaine, tomatoes, white onions, and pastrami sautéed in Olive oil, chopped green onions and chopped garlic." She started walking to an empty booth at the far end of the diner. "It started picking up this morning around breakfast and hasn't let up. We got a few couples who had breakfast, left, and came back for lunch."

Rick whistled as he sat down opposite Barbara. "Sounds like tourist."

Sarah nodded. "Most of the folks are shopping the mall. Three said some friends told them about the Lo'tion."

"Good friends," Rick grunted.

"I'd say," Barbara replied. "I think I know what I want." She puckered her lips and smiled.

Rick said, "But what about food?"

Barbara launched a kick at Rick whose legs were not there.

He laughed and kicked back. He felt her shin and was satisfied he probably gave her a bruise.

Barbara barely flinched. She lowered her head and squinted her eyes.

Rick swallowed hard, turned pale and thought, 'Oh, shit! I'm doomed.'

Barbara smiled, satisfied that Rick got the message.

Sarah coughed. "Are you two secretly married?"

"This is what happens when partners work together for years."

Rick said, "Sarah, I think I'll be hanging out with you for a while. I need a witness."

Barbara gave Rick the middle finger. "He'll have a Pastrami baguette, too. Hold the onions for him . . ."

"Hey!" Rick interrupted. "I think I can order my own . . ."

Barbara turned her head toward Sarah.

Sarah nodded. "No onions for Rick." She smiled and walked away to place the order.

Rick watched as Sarah approached the kitchen door. He noted how her skirt hugged tightly around her hips.

"Tiger, down." Barbara joked.

Rick slowly tore his eyes away from Sarah as she disappeared behind the kitchen door. "What?"

Barbara smiled, "You two getting serious?"

His smile was faint.

Approvingly Barbara nodded. "Good. I noticed you stopped consuming gum."

Rick thought for a moment. He searched his jacket pockets. Barb was right. The urge for smoking was gone. Damn her. One more thing she would rub his nose in.

***

The trip to Mr. Donald J Martin's home took about two hours. Muhammad had insisted the meeting be face to face. They had to show Mr. Martin the articles in hardcopy, the photos, the graphs, and reports. He had to listen to some of the recordings and he had to read some of the emails. He was old-fashioned and insisted on feeling paper or listening to speech. He signed contracts with a pen and paid his employees with a personal check. Payroll dealt with taxes of course, but he wanted to be known to his employees as a Boss who paid them out of his own pocket, at least as much out of his own pocket as a billionaire could.

Mr. Martin had been nice enough to send Muhammad and Walter a limo. Walt hoped they could leave that way instead of having to call for a cab, which was quite possible. Mr. Martin, when pissed, had been known to show his guests the door and walk away without any parting words.

Walter stepped out of the Limo. The long winding path from the front gate to the main house took about 15 minutes. During that time Walter marveled at the sheer waste of money. Tall oak trees lined either side of the path toward the house with the road paved in tan-yellow bricks. Several years ago, Mr. Martin's oldest daughter finally married. Forrest was there. Muhammad and Vannessa covered the story. Vannessa did photos while Muhammad wrote the article. The story ran with the title, "A Road Paved in Honey." And it looked the part.

"Please follow me," one of Martin's many staffers said while gesturing toward the main house.

Walter walked up the long flight of stairs to two tall massive front doors. "Seriously," he said out loud.

Muhammad nodded, "Money is money. Wait until you see the inside."

"Welcome to the Estate, Good Sirs." Said a man dressed in a black jacket with rather long tails and black creased trousers. His white shirt seemed too white. It seemed to glow in the sun light.

Walter had to shake his head to snap out of the obvious daze he was in. The doorman smiled. The effect always took the first timer by surprise.

"Welcome to the Home," the Doorman said.

Walter nodded. He stepped through the doorway and was hit with a sudden case of agoraphobia. The inner foyer was expansive. Tall thick columns supported vaulted ceilings at least twenty feet high. The floor made of a translucent reflective material sheened to mimic a deep canyon. "You want me to walk across that?"

Muhammad laughed. "The first time I walked

through those doors I nearly passed out. As I said. Money is money."

Someone softly coughed behind Walter. "Please follow me."

Walter and Muhammad followed the man through a passage way off from the main path. The corridor took them through several turns to eventually open up into a modest sized room. Each wall was covered with books. A solid oak desk was nestled in between two tall solid wood bookshelves.

Donald J Martin stood up from the desk. He walked around it and greeted Muhammad warmly with a firm handshake. He turned to Walter. "Mr. Kincaid, so very nice to meet you."

Walter took his handshake. The man's hand was cool, almost too cool for his liking. It felt odd to the touch, but Walt returned the firm grip.

"Please, have a seat gentlemen."

Muhammad sat. "Thank you, sir." He handed a wad of thick envelopes to a staffer waiting.

The staffer accepted the material and stepped over to Mr. Martin's desk. He reached into the large envelope and pulled the SolidState Drives out first. Next came the plastic back binder notebooks. He handed those to Martin. The SolidState Drives he inserted into the appropriate slots on the side of the desk.

Martin sat back in his chair. He listened to the audios while reading through the notebooks.

Muhammad and Walter waited quietly. It took Martin about an hour to finish reading all the transcripts, reports, emails, and articles. He looked over to Muhammad, who looked over to the Staffer. The man nodded, turned and walked toward a wet bar off in the corner of the office. A few minutes later he came back with two drinks. A Rum and Coke for Muhammad and a Cape Cod for Walter.

Walter accepted the drink with wide eyes. "How?" He whispered.

Muhammad shrugged, "ESP, maybe. Enjoy and relax. Food is next."

Walter frowned. "How wou . . ."

Another Staffer walked in with a small table. Assorted fruit, vegetables and small ham, turkey, tofu, and pastrami sandwiches adorned the top. She left the small table between the two and walked out.

Muhammad shrugged, smiled, and popped a red grape into his mouth.

Martin cleared his throat.

Walter and Muhammad looked up.

"You know I'm on the board?"

Both men nodded.

"You also know I have a lot of money invested in Forever Live?"

Walter swallowed the thick lump that formed in the middle of his throat. Where was the man going with this he thought?

"And you come here with information that could bring the company to near bankruptcy." Martin slammed his fist onto the desk.

Walter and Muhammad flinched.

"What the fuck is wrong with this picture?!?" Martin yelled.

Walter's heart sank. The man was going to kill the story and toss them out.

Martin took a deep breath and scratched underneath his chin. He gave the two men a hard stare.

Muhammad looked away but Walter locked gaze. After a minute Martin smiled. "Run it," he said.

Walter blurted, "But, sir, you can't . . . wait . . . what?"

"Run the series."

Muhammad frowned. "As is, sir? No changes?"

"None. That arrogant son of a bitch will get what he deserves. He muscled me out of the chair, so this is payback. The morning this hits the Net I'll call an emergency meeting." He laughed out loud. "Can't wait to see that smug look wiped off his face."

Muhammad nodded. "Understood, sir."

"Damn, this is going to be bitter sweet." Martin reached over and pulled a remote phone from its cradle. He dialed a number and waited a few seconds. "Ted, me Martin. You still got controlling stock?" He listened for a few minutes. "I got something to boost your ratings. What?!? How'd you get the info?" He covered the mike part. "One of his guys received a packet last night. Had lots of info on Forever Life and Forrest." He placed the phone back to his ear. "Yeah, same thing. My guys have worked the angle already. We release tomorrow morning . . . yeah . . . okay . . . not really . . . Sounds like a good idea . . . we can do that." He covered the mike. "Are we ready to release in one hour?"

Muhammad went wide-eyed. He stammered a second, thought about it, then nodded.

Martin smiled, "Yeah . . . yeah . . . that works. Hey, you're heading up to Juno tomorrow? Wanna catch the race? I got the new deck built. You can see the entire course . . . good. Meet you up there in twelve." He hung the phone up. "Well, Muhammad, Global Informational

News is going live in an hour. Make it happen."

Muhammad and Walter nodded.

A Staffer walked up to the men and gestured toward the door.

Walter nearly stumbled out of the chair. "Thank you, sir."

Martin looked up from his computer screen, nodded and went back to viewing.

Walter had to hurry to catch up to Muhammad. 'Oh boy oh boy," was his thought. This is gonna get ugly.

Interim Chapter

Prax stood in front of Omega's chamber. "Is this the best course of action?"

Mike answered. "With the current parameters in play? It is. Events have been put in place that there is a conclusion, which may require his strength. He has been reconditioned."

"Will he be independent?"

Mike paused for a moment. "He will be."

Pete Walker woke up with a start. He wasn't supposed to be here. Not this place. Not this time. He reached up and felt the oxygen mask tightly over his mouth, nose, and eyes. His hands seemed strangely oversized through the green liquid. Then he remembered he still wasn't supposed to be here. He couldn't. Damn! Another failure. He had died, now he was awake. Pete took a deep breath and tested his eyes. The filtered light had a green tint to it, so the stinging shock of using his eyes for the first time wasn't so overly painful, just maybe annoying. He took another deep breath and tested his hands. Each finger flexed, but they looked grossly huge. Maybe something happened during the cloning process. Hopefully, he thought, he wouldn't be some hulking monstrosity. He looked up at a blinking display board over his head. It flashed "Purge in progress. Please standby." He looked around and spotted the readout displays to his right. Little monitors flashed and displayed numbers and text. One display was counting down. Another was scrolling odd bits of information, like "Family is important!", "Protect family at all cost!", "You have the ability to save lives!", "It's time to leave. Prepare." That he thought odd. He looked over at the monitor that was displaying a countdown of sorts. Then he remembered. "Purge in progress." He looked up and saw two metal rings. He grabbed them. Seconds later he felt the floor underneath his feet vanish. The green tinted fluid slipped away from his eyesight. He remembered the process now. He waited until the fluid completely drained. The system would cycle through several procedures. Purge was first, wash was second. Release was third. He counted to three and the floor came back. Seconds later the container he was in filled with some clear fluid – water he thought. It was warm and turbulent, like a washing machine. Minutes ticked by as the chamber filled, circulated, and drained several times. The little countdown display kept track and reminded him he was not the original. Intellectually he understood he was not the original. Waking up in a thick green goo fluid reinforced that, too. When the countdown display reached zero he was hit with a blast of hot air. It whirled around him rapidly. He was dry in seconds. He lowered himself far enough to feel the grid floor and tested his legs. Strong, firm, stable. He let go of the overhead rings and with his weight fully supported by his feet he unsnapped his harness. He looked out through the chamber glass and saw an android staring at him. Had he been asleep that long? He heard a loud audible click and the glass door whooshed up out of sight.

Pete stepped out and felt a chill.

He looked down at the android, which seemed strange. From what he could tell it had to have been at least 6 feet tall.

Prax looked up and said, "Welcome to your new life . . . Omega."

Chapter 18

Kent made Forrest wait 30 minutes before he walked into the Diner. He had a TransStrip stuck just behind his left ear. Mike could talk to him via bone induction and pick up any sound he heard – near or extremely far. Sarah spotted him, each arm covered in plates with Baguette Pastrami sandwiches. "Hey George! Over here!"

Kent kept the smile on his face. With George's memories he recognized the hostess, Sarah. She was a pretty middle-aged woman who could have easily starred in a porn video featuring MILFs.

"I was worried. Are you okay?"

He nodded, "Yeah, Sarah. How goes it?"

She smiled and visibly relaxed. "Let me drop these off, then I can scare up a seat."

Kent spotted Forrest sitting at a booth. A slender man with dark hair sat at the edge of the booth with Forrest in the middle. "Sarah, I'm here to see an associate." Kent pointed his chin toward Forrest.

Sarah turned. "Him? Sure Darlin'. He and his friend had been waiting for 30 minutes. Didn't know you were the one. I'll get your order in a moment."

Kent nodded and headed to the Horseshoe shaped

booth.

Troy stood up as Kent approached. He could see some resemblance. Not identical, but enough to think the two men could be related.

Kent eyed Troy as he stood. Nice gesture he thought. A man with some culture. He reached the booth and sat.

Troy sat back down.

Forrest never moved. On one level he felt a connection. This man was his brother and yet he was the enemy – his enemy me. On a deeper level he hated the man. No ties, no obligations or responsibilities. He came into the world when technology was just starting to cross that fine line of 'how special' to 'it's all magic'.

Sarah stepped up to the tablet, "What can I finally get you two?" She looked at Troy and Forrest.

Forrest spoke. "What's the special?"

"Today it's Pastrami on French Baguette."

"Make it three . . ."

Kent coughed. "Sourdough for me, Sarah."

Sarah did a double take. "You feverish? Sourdough?"

Kent nodded. "Today I'd like to do a change up." He shrugged and closed his eyes briefly.

Sarah smiled. "Sure, Darlin'. We need that every now and then. Drinks?"

"Water for me." Kent said.

Forrest said, "Same for us."

Kent smiled. "He has a neck, which should contain a voice box. Can't he speak?"

Troy said, "I can speak. Water would be fine, ma'am, thanks."

Sarah pursed her lips. She thought George had worse company over the years, but these two seemed off – not quite comfortable. "Water for all." She turned and left.

"Well, Alpha . . ."

"That is not my name," Forrest said with clinched teeth.

"I didn't say it as a name. I said it as a title. There are other names I could use, but Alpha is better."

Forest cocked an eyebrow.

"You'd rather I call you Fucker? Bastard, Asshole?"

"I'd rather you call me by my name brother, Forrest."

"I got too much of George's memory to give you that much respect . . . Alpha. You're lucky I even acknowledge you."

Forrest's face scrunched up in anger. He was about to unleash a torrent of insults when Sarah appeared with the water.

Sarah carefully placed the glasses of iced water in front of each man. Kent nodded and said 'Thanks,' but he didn't look at her. The other two remained silent. She noticed the dark hair one staring intensely at George. She decided this wasn't going to turn out well. "Would you gentlemen like something else while Mel fixes your sandwiches?"

Kent focused on Forrest. "I'm good."

Forrest said nothing, but Troy took his eyes off Kent and said with a smile, "No thanks, ma'am. We're good. But thank you for asking."

Sarah furrowed here eyebrows and nodded.

***

Thompson flashed his hand over the side console. The center display flashed to a new image. Rick,

Barbara, Kovik, two reps, Keller Parks and Meg Wilson, from the DA watched.

The first image showed Pete Walker strapped to a table, sedated. Someone in a Level 3 Hazmat suit stepped into camera range.

Keller was a tall brunette with long hair and long legs. She was the DA. Meg, assistant DA, was about two feet shorter, small but solid built. She had blonde hair with dark roots. Keller asked, "Has this been authenticated?"

Thompson nodded. "Confirmed. All the vids have."

Pete screamed and nearly everyone flinched. Meg looked away from the display.

"And we confirmed that to be Peter Walker?"

Thompson nodded. "Face recognition."

"And they recorded this?"

"This vid was hacked . . ."

Meg turned to face Thompson. "Forever Life was hacked? The NSA couldn't do it."

Smekhov spoke up. "Probably an inside job. The PixConfirm code match the checksum. This vid came from inside Forever Life. From the buildings continuous record feed. That vid was saved as it was happening. It is not a copy in the sense of a copy. There are no other PixConfirm. "

Keller's left eyebrow raised. "You can testify to that?"

"Numbers don't lie. Having one of their Security stations in here couldn't have gotten a better vid."

"What about the source?"

Thompson, Anosov, and Smekhov shrugged.

Thompson said, "It was delivered by a special carrier."

Rick spoke up, "He was sent a key to a locker at the station with a thick envelope of cash and a note. No fingerprints and everything was void of any DNA . . ."

". . . Any?" Keller interrupted.

Thompson said, "None . . ."

Anosov said, "Nada . . ."

Smekhov finished, "Zip."

Thompson shrugged. "Seriously, the only DNA found was cross-contam from the carrier and the surrounding area. Even the paper can't be traced."

Meg asked, "Ink?"

"Heat thermal printing. Laser burn."

There was another scream in the background.

Keller said, "WTF."

Anosov said, "Rapid genetic change."

She pointed to the screen, "That's disgusting!"

Pete's arm had ballooned to three times its size in seconds. The person in the Hazmat suit stuck the bicep with a long thin needle. Seconds later the arm shrank to normal, but Pete went into convulsions. A moment later he stopped moving. The Hazmat figure slowly walked over to a panel of buttons and monitors. He looked at a monitor for several seconds, reached out and pressed a button. Pete's body jerked several times. The individual waited a few more seconds, pressed the button again. Pete's body jerked several more times. The individual stepped away and leaned over Pete's head. His body obstructed the view.

Keller asked, "What's the time stamp?"

"Eight years ago." Thompson said. He waved his arm across the console and the vid disappeared. "We have about two thousand hours of vids. And the emails — hundreds of pages. From the documents, another five thousand pages. It looks like Forever Life is working on a drug to make phenotype changes in a matter of days . . ."

Barbara blurted, "That's crazy!"

Thompson hovered his hands, palms up, and acted like he were weighing two items. "Maybe, but think about it. You can change your hair color, texture, length, thickness, anything in several days. You want canine teeth? Swallow the pill or take some injection or both. Need a bigger butt?" He paused when his eyes drifted toward Barbara's rear. "Now it's a choice." He quickly looked up.

Barbara kept a straight face, but the urge to cold cock Thompson was strong.

"Forever Life . . ."

"Is nuts!" Rick stressed. "Pete died over fifteen years ago. I was only several feet away from him. I id'ed the body."

Keller nodded. "Okay, okay. Clearly Forever Life has been working above the law. I'll ask for a Search Warrant. It's gonna be a hard sell."

Rick spoke up. "Seriously? With what we just saw? When the DOJ gets wind of this they'll want a piece of the action, if not all of it."

Keller replied, "Judge Thorpe is on call this week."

"Oh." Rick said. "Fuck. He ain't gonna bite the hand that's been feeding him."

"Maybe, maybe not. I can always take it to the DOJ, but I want this in our court first. We need this take down." Keller replied. She shrugged.

Rick thought election season was another two years away.

Anosov said, "Thorpe is on record for openly

condemning cloning. You know - God, creation, and the whole bag of chips are lady in dip."

Smekhov punched him in the arm.

"What? All I'm saying is that you can't get any more conservative than Thorpe. I think he'll sign . . ."

Rick's Mobile went off. The ringtone was a cackle – his ex-wife. "One sec." He pulled it out and looked at the caller id. It was Sarah. A smile formed on his face. He cleared his throat and he gave himself some distance from the group. "Pearl, speaking." He hoped he sounded professional. "How can . . ."

"Rick, this is Sarah. George is here."

"Hey Sarah, how is . . . wait . . . what?"

"George is here."

Rick placed the device against his shoulder. "George is at the Lo'tion."

He placed the mobile back to his ear. "Sarah, we'll be there in twenty minutes. For Goddess sake, keep cool and keep him there."

"They got another 10 minutes before Mel finishes making the sandwiches."

"They?" He asked.

"A Guy in a very expensive suit with male eye candy next to him."

"A Red head?"

"The eye-candy? He has jet black hair. The guy in the suit has the red hair."

'OMG,' Rick thought. "On the way. See you in a few." He clicked off. "I think Forrest is meeting with George."

Smekhov held her hand out in front of Anosov. "Give."

Anosov reached into his inside jacket pocket and pulled out a Secured CashCard. He slapped it in

Smekhov's hand.

The Card disappeared with a smug Smekhov smiling.

***

Troy coughed. Forrest and Kent had been staring at one another for the last three minutes. Sarah stopped by once to ask if everything was okay. Troy nodded and flashed her a toothy smile.

Kent broke the silence first. "You wanted this meeting."

Forrest took a deep breath. "Brother . . ."

"Of which I'm not happy to be."

Forrest's neck muscles tightened. He sucked in his lips. "Transgenetics is safe."

"Safe now, but how many of us died getting to this point?"

Forrest remained silent.

"You used one of us as a Guinea Pig . . ."

Forrest held up a hand.

Kent kept his voice low. ". . . don't try and bullshit me. I've seen the vids on Pete Three. You murdered him and you got nerve to sit in front of me and act like you're a victim of bad PR." He scrunched his face up in disgust. "How, how can I possible forgive you for that? Shut the fuck up you bastard I'm still talking and you got little to atone your sins. I will do everything I can to take you and Forever Death down. Your Transgenocide is the wrong answer." Kent exhaled.

Forrest measured Kent with a careful eye. Atrocities against who? Another clone? This was the big picture. Global change. Universal change. Everyone would be affected. Disease, illness, crippling handicaps erased.

Couldn't he see it? This is a service to human kind. This is the needs of the many, not the few. Epic. "You're a fool. Now you shut the fuck up. It's my turn . . ."

Kent leaned forwarded.

"No . . . you had your rant. You, George, all the others and Pete lacked vision. Your myopic view wasn't going to liberate the world anytime soon. Short-sighted, narrow-minded bullshit. All of it. I'm offering the world, the world, liberation from everything. Everything. Not just cosmetic, but everything. You sit there and try to threaten me? How fucking dare you. You're just another piece of cheap life, clone. Three months' worth of wasted time."

Sarah stepped up with a forced smile. She placed the sandwiches on the table, dropped napkins next to each plate, and backed away slowly. She overheard, like others in the diners, some of the argument. In all these years she assumed she knew George. She liked him. He seemed nice. Sure he had arguments with Joe, but Joe was an asshole. But this man he was talking to? This was different. This was raw.

Forrest slammed his hand down on the table. "I should never have come. You're just as hard-headed as George."

Kent leaned forward. "You pompous sanctimonious ass. The base gene is ours . . ."

"Corrected."

"Bullshit. It has not been corrected. It's the same as day one."

"How would you know?"

"I got access to everything."

Shocked, Forrest sat speechless. He frowned. "Everything?"

Kent leaned back. "Everything. Minute one. Understand? Minute one."

Forrest clenched his teeth. His lips stretched thin showing his incisors and canines. "What do you want?"

Kent leaned forward. He lowered his head and looked Forrest in the eye. "Abandon Transgenetics . . ."

Forrest sucked in air loudly.

". . . or at least come up with a way to use the Host's DNA as the base."

"Impossible!" Forrest spat out. "That would price the treatment out of range to 85% of the population."

"And?"

Forrest shook his head. "Transgenetics is for the masses . . ."

"Who will line the pockets on shareholders and increase your wealth. And I know about the hidden sequence."

"What hidden sequence?"

Kent cocked his head to the right and smiled. "Created in his image."

Forrest sat in silence for a moment. "What are you talking about?"

"You sick Fuck. Repeated usage eventually changes the facial phenotype. That's the base gene used."

Forrest slipped out from the booth. "I'm done with you, clone. You better enjoy this meal."

"You threatening me?"

Forrest laughed and caught the attention of everyone in the Diner. He stepped away from the booth with Troy following close behind. As he passed Sarah he handed her a wad of Fed notes. "That should cover the meal and tip."

Sarah quickly counted out several hundred Fed

notes. She pulled out two twenty notes and started to hand the wad back, but it was too late. Forrest and Troy were on the other side of the door.

Kent stared at his sandwich. The war was on. Forrest would try to murder him now. That was clear. He avoided eye contact with mostly everyone in the Diner. At times he knew Forrest and himself had been carelessly loud, but that was good - Witnesses. And Witnesses meant allies. Kent softly said, "Mike? Any news?" He absently rubbed at the induction strip behind his ear.

Mike said, "The van with some of Forrest's Security Units is headed to your location."

"I think it's time to leave then."

"Two detectives are also approaching the Diner."

Kent raised an eyebrow, "Really?"

"They want to question you, or I should clarify. They want to question George."

Kent took a bite from his sandwich. He chewed slowly and decided that sourdough was also a good choice. "Can you delay the Security Units?"

"Already done."

"How much time do we have?"

"As much as you need. Security Units have been taken care of."

"May I ask how?" Kent asked after swallowing another bite.

"You may ask," Mike said.

Kent took two more bites before saying, "How?"

Mike appreciated the position he was in. If he had been human he would have laughed. "You asked, Kent."

Kent smiled. So, Mike really is human after all he thought. "Understood."

Mike concluded the laugh would have been a very

satisfying one.

***

Barbara pulled the car into the Lo'tion's parking area. Her mind still racing over what they saw down the road. They would have made it sooner but the accident required they stop and offer assistance. She looked over to Rick. He was going through his own thoughts. How do you explain a heavy cargo van crushed? With no witnesses? Not even camera surveillance coverage. Every single camera that could have seen the accident malfunctioned, switched off, or had been pointed in a different direction. What were the odds she thought? The cameras were working now, but at that very moment of the accident . . . nothing. And, the Security Units in the van. All crushed like squeezed clay with their heads removed and backup recorders missing. Now they sat in the car, engine still running. Division had dispatched a team and Thompson and his Group were on the way. She and Rick only left when a patrol car, which heard the call over the comm, pulled up. She turned the engine off. "Ready?"

Rick nodded. He hoped George and Forrest were still there.

***

Kent was two bites into the second half of his sandwich when he heard Sarah.

"Detectives! How are you?" She said. "We're a bit full. Care to wait for a seat?"

Rick cleared his throat. "That would be nice, but

maybe you can help us?"

"Yes?"

He pulled out the Pic of George he showed her a week ago. "Have you seen this person before?"

Sarah was glad Rick pulled the pic out. She so hated calling him. She pretty much felt like she ratted George out. "Oh, yeah, I have. Is he in trouble or something?"

Kent concealed his smile by taking another bite.

Rick said, "Not at all. We just have some questions. He may be able to help us with an on-going investigation." Total bullshit spiel flashed through Rick's mind. 'Oscar performance!'

"In that case, he's over here." She walked toward Kent with Rick and Barbara following. When she reached the table she said, "George, sorry to bother you, but . . ."

Kent turned around. "It's okay, Sarah. I heard. Thanks for making sure things were cool." He stood up and faced Rick and Barbara. "Detectives. How may I be of assistance?"

Barbara eyed him carefully. He looked like Pete Walker.

Rick could only stare. This was the face, albeit a little younger, he remembered from more than fifteen years ago.

Mike said through the Induction strip, "They know you are not George. They've seen some of the Pete Three vids."

Kent, to his credit, kept a straight face. Mike had to have sent some vids to the Police. No doubt he was holding out on what secret agenda he had running. Kent was beginning to think there really was more to Mike. "Join me, please." He gestured to the empty space around the booth. The two sandwiches were still there. "Have lunch with me."

Sarah said, "His guest left early. The sandwiches are paid for."

Mel yelled from the back, "Order!"

Sarah touched Kent lightly on the shoulder and left.

Barbara and Rick looked at one another.

"Their names are Rick Pearl and Barbara Tipper." Mike said.

"Please", Kent started, "Detectives Pearl and Tipper. We have much to discuss."

Rick said, "How did . . ."

Kent shrugged, "ESP." His smile was genuine.

They hesitated.

"The sandwiches are delicious."

"Who are you?" Rick asked as he sat down.

"My name is Kent. May I call you Rick, Rick?"

The Detective nodded. "Who is this?" He slid the Pic over.

"George Walker, my brother."

"Brother?" Barbara said. She lowered her voice. "And, not a clone?"

"Depends on your definition . . ." He took another bite. "Forrest is the only true clone. I'm not. And no genetic testing in the world will disprove that."

Barbara leaned forward. She had half a sandwich in her hand and after giving it a good sniff she tasted a small edge. She paused and took a bigger bite. "You know about Forever Life?"

"Of course, we were created to fight Forrest." He sighed and looked toward a corner of the ceiling. "I'm the last of the Pete look-alikes."

Barbara swallowed and took another bite, normal

sized. "This is good!"

Rick scowled, "We're not here to eat."

"I'm hungry. And it's paid for."

"And we have a case . . ."

"To solve." Kent finished. "I figured that much."

"Was Forrest here?" Rick asked.

Kent nodded. "His sandwich is in front of you." He smiled. "He didn't like what I had to say and left."

Rick stared down at the sandwich. He liked pastrami. He caught Sarah's eye and waved her over.

"Yes, hon?" She said.

He liked the sound of that, but she said Hon to everyone. "A Bell's, please."

She nodded and looked at Barbara.

"Are the drinks covered too?"

Sarah nodded.

"The Ten Credit Shake then. Kiwi Lime."

"Good choice. My favorite, too. And you George?"

"I'll have a Bell's, too."

Sarah turned and left.

Kent noticed Rick watching her retreat intensely. "You asked her out yet?"

Rick snapped out of his daze. "What?"

"You asked her out yet?"

Rick frowned. "WTF. You, too?"

Barbara stifled a laughed. "Look, this is weird. We've only known you for all of five minutes and you seem to be personable."

Kent visibly relaxed. "A common enemy usually creates a united front and . . ."

". . . Are we really after the same ends?" Barbara asked.

"I think so, though our methods might differ." He

took the last bite of his sandwich.

Sarah dropped off the drinks and waited on a new customer.

"You gonna blow yourself up?" Rick asked while chewing his bite.

"Not me, but George had six years of frustration. Maybe if this doesn't pan out soon, I might have to consider that route."

"Why? Why do this?" Barbara asked.

Kent took a sip of his Bell's. He savored the pleasant taste with just that right amount of bitter aftertaste. "You saw the vids?"

Rick and Barbara nodded.

"There are also other reasons. Transgenetics will eventually cause inbreeding, that is, if it is available to the masses at an affordable price. Plus there is an Easter egg in the sequence."

"Such as?" Rick asked.

Kent smiled and took another swallow of Bell's. "Good choice, Rick. I like this beer."

"The Easter egg?"

"I like my face, but think of it. A world where we all look the same. Global equality, a solution to racism, the only thing left to discriminate is belief and not looks? A path to utopia?"

Barbara said, "Wait . . . what? Are you talking about a drug?"

"Yeah. See a Doctor. Talk to a Genetic Consultant, take a series of pills, go into a coma, and days later magic. A new you. Literally. It is big, but he's going about it the cheapest way possible."

"And that is?" Rick asked.

"Using a base genetic code . . ." The beer went down

smoothly as he took another swallow. "Ours."

"What exactly do you mean a new you?"

Kent looked Rick in the eye. "You like your eye color? Want to change it? How about your height? A little too thick around the mid-section? Hate your hair? Your voice? Your face? Flat butt, big butt? No chest, too much chest? Bad memory? Cancer? Hay fever? The cold. We are talking epic changes here. Nothing will eventually be left untouched. Nothing."

"What's wrong with that?"

Kent finished his beer. It was time for him to go. "Using your own DNA, nothing. Using a base DNA everything. Short term it would be fine, but long term and inclusive of a huge population? Inbreeding or Sterility – your choice. It all comes down to profit. Make a hundred million or make hundreds of billions? And that would be his cut." He picked up a napkin and dabbed at his lips. "It's been fun, but I have to leave."

Rick grabbed Kent's arm as he started rising. "Sorry, but I'd like you to talk to the DA."

Kent brushed the hand off. "Am I being charged? If so, on what?"

Barbara blurted out "Conspiracy, the act of committing conspiracy."

Kent laughed. "Seriously?"

"This is too big for you to walk away." Rick stressed. Then suddenly he was hit in the face with a piece of shortbread cake.

Barbara said, "What the . . ." before being hit with an apple pie.

Rick wiped his eyes in time to see a short man jump up on a table.

Marty tossed the cake first. He giggled as Rick's head snapped back from the impact and his partner was taken by complete surprise. Pearl threw the pie at Barbara. It hit dead center nose. He jumped up onto his table and yelled, "Food fight!"

A moment later Rick and Barbara stood alone save for Sarah, who was not touched, and two other wait staffs were covered in food. Mel stepped out from the Kitchen. He was a large stocky man with thinning hair and a dark complexion from over tanning. He yelled, "What in the hell is going on?"

The entire dining area was awash with food.

Sarah shrugged and walked over to Rick.

Rick spat out a piece of cake. "WTF." Then his phone beep. He answered. "Pearl here."

It was the chief. The Search Warrant was ready.

Chapter 19

The Security team missed check in. That worried Forrest. He sat at his desk and checked an anonymous MesBox. Nothing. The van and the units were unmarked and comfortably untraceable. Only an unfortunate and careless cross-contamination would tie in one of his contractors, who could eventually point to his desk.

Troy chimed the door. He chimed several more times within several seconds.

Forrest, irritated, pressed the enter button.

Troy hurried over. The look on his face told Forrest something was wrong. "Sir, channel 7. Important. All bad news."

Strange. Forrest had never seen Troy flustered. He clicked the main display screen. It was a 190 inch flat screen unit secured against a vacant portion of the far wall. The display flicked on and caught the newscaster in mid speech.

" . . . CEO Forrest Taylor is alleged in a conspiracy to release a highly controversial drug known as Transgenetics. Currently, set for Human trials, the FDA has placed a hold on the go ahead . . ."

Forrest's heart sank. "No, no, no, no, NO!"

"Sir, more bad news." He handed Forrest a tablet.

The Watcher Group released a special report on the dangers of Gene Therapy. A headline article id'ed key players in Transgenetics development. It accused Forever Life of conducting illegal deadly human trials. Several photos showed Pete Walker's face twisted in agony.

Forrest got up and went to the window. He could see the flashing lights of Division vehicles convoying to the main gate. Forrest made a mental note to stop all donations to Thorpe's future campaign.

The lead car stopped. Someone got out and approached the guard station. Seconds later the officer had the guard in a choke hold while another one worked the controls to open the large steel gate. Another officer approached the two and slapped handcuffs on the guard. The convoy resumed its way to the main entrance of the building.

Forrest's phone rang. The caller id said 'Martin'. Bastard he thought. Forrest sat at his desk. "Troy, handle Division please."

Troy's facial expression said it all. Doomed. He nodded and left.

Forrest picked up the handset. "Donald. . ."

Martin replied, "Forrest. The board held an emergency meeting. Sorry to have to give you the news. We voted you out. Under clause 12 section 4 item a3 you will not receive a parachute option . . ."

"You set me up, you bastard. How could you?"

Martin replied, "You may blame me, but it was your own arrogance that did it. You have eight hours to take what you need. How could you take us down this . . . ?"

"Take us? You signed off on Transgenetics!"

"But not torture and murder."

Forrest remained silent.

Martin continued, "You took us down a road that'll cut deep in profit. Tomorrow morning the Exchanges will open. Every investor will sell. We'll drop and you are to blame. You no longer have access to company files . . ."

Forrest tapped out several commands on his computer. All came up 'Access denied.' He hung up — no use in talking. He walked over to the wet bar and poured a half glass of Cognac. Lime juice, sparkling water, and several black olives completed the drink. He walked out of his office, passed Troy's unoccupied desk. His private elevator would not respond to his palm press so he was forced to use the public lift. He pressed Garage PRV and was thankful that the elevator made the trip without anyone requesting a stop. Today he would take one of his private cars home. 'Sid' he thought. His lawyer. He's going to have to call Sid. Sid was the best and could have gotten Jesus out of a jam if he had been there. Several Security Units were waiting near his car. He sighed. Good, at least they're allowing me to have some protection on the way home. As he got nearer to his car one unit stepped out and blocked his way.

"Please, sir. I have to ask you to wait."

Forrest scowled. "Wait for what?"

The unit said, "You are to be held until Head of Security has a chance to clear you."

Clear . . . clear me! What the fuck! Clear me!"

The other units stepped forward. A second unit said, "Sir, display any further acts of aggression and you will be pacified."

Forrest was shocked. "Aggression! I'll . . ."

The unit stepped closer.

Forrest closed his mouth. And held his hands up to his chest with palms facing out.

The unit stopped.

Forrest waited ten minutes until the evening Chief of Security arrived with several other units.

"Sorry, sir. But the Chairman . . ."

"I'm the Chairma . . ."

"The Interim Chairman said to search you for any company property. Please spread your legs and lift up your arms, sir."

A now red faced Forrest complied. The search was quick but degrading. Afterward he got into his car.

"Sir, the main entrance is choked full of reporters. I suggest the service entrance."

Forrest bite his bottom lip, nodded, and sped toward the service entrance. Disgraced. Tears welled up in his eyes and started streaming down his cheek. He pulled up next to the intercom/Gate access unit. His card wouldn't work. He tried several more times. Then he pressed the call button.

A minute later a voice came over the unit's speakers, "Yes?"

"This is Forrest Taylor. I need to leave."

The gate remained closed.

"I need to leave. Open the gate, god damn it!"

The gate remained closed.

Forrest roared and punched at the ceiling several times. He took a deep breath and begrudgingly said, "Please. I just want to get home."

After several seconds the gate opened. Forrest

drove up the path to the main road. Several Division cars were blocking the intersection. Forrest stopped as an Officer approached him.

A detective walked up to the car. "Mr. Taylor, please turn off the engine and step out."

Forrest let the window down. "Detective, why are you stopping me? I'm a citizen."

The detective nodded, "Understood, sir. But I still need you to step out."

Forrest put his window back up. "How dare they!" He yelled to no one in particular while punching in the number to Sid. "I'll sue the company, I'll sue Division. Everyone!"

A deep voice answered. "Fineburg, speaking."

"Sid! This is Forrest, I need . . ."

"Forrest, Forrest," Sid interrupted, "Where are you?"

The detective knocked on the car window. He moved his lips but Forrest heard nothing.

"In my car. I'm being detained. Division officers and a Detective are blocking my way home."

The detective knocked on the window harder. It thumped and startled Forrest.

"Sid, this is a disaster."

"I heard."

"You what? Heard? How?"

"Forrest, it's all over the news and the Net feeds. Is it true?"

Forrest pursed his lips.

"Is it true? God help you if it is."

"Some." He finally said.

"Sheesh, Forrest."

"You can fix this."

"Forrest, look. This is not looking good. You need to turn yourself in and . . ."

A very loud thump hit the window. The Officers were using a battering ram. Thump, thump!

"Sid! They're trying to break into my car! Call someone!"

"Forrest, turn yourself in . . ."

"The fuck I will!"

"You have too. You're a private citizen away from the company."

Then it hit Forrest. Out in the open, vulnerable. He had no Security Units for protection. "Sid, I'm scared."

"I'm making a call to the Mayor and the Division Chief, but it's gonna take time. Doing it now before it's too late."

There were several more thumps. Forrest considered running but that would have been dumb. He turned off the engine and lowered the window a bit. "Okay, I'm stepping out. Please don't hurt me."

The Officers backed up allowing the car door to open.

"Sid, for God's sake, hurry." Then he said, "Car, record mode."

The vehicle beeped. A computer voice said loudly, "Vehicle is in record mode. Vehicle is in record mode."

Forrest only hoped that would be enough to guarantee not being shot by a Division Officer. "I'm stepping out."

The Detective let him clear the car. He took a deep breath. "Mr. Taylor, I have a Warrant for your arrest."

"What's the charge?"

"Fraud. Kidnapping. Assault. Murder. Please turn around and place your hands on top of your head."

Forrest started to turn around when his knees buckled.

The Detective caught him and pressed him hard against his car. He placed restraining straps around Forrest's wrists.

It was a nightmare Forrest thought. A true nightmare. He looked up and saw a few helicopters hovering overhead. Three were Division, the other half dozen were from News Agencies.

***

Prax had finished passing out the bags of Popcorn and drinks when Mike started the compilation. He had been recording all the major News channels and spliced the best of the broadcasts together. A live feed picture was nestled in the corner of the large display when someone yelled. "Look, they got him cornered."

The feed played out the moment Forrest's car was stopped by Division, the battering ram on the window, and Forrest finally arrested. The display zoomed in close on a teary eyed face as the detective placed restraining bands around his wrists.

Marty said, "Now what? This is over, right?"

Mike said, "Not quite. I've established IDs for everyone as well as history, medical records, residencies, education, everything that will allow you to function as regular citizens."

Pearl asked, "What about work?"

"Taken care of. The documents Division has in their possession financial records that shows Forever Life had been paying you a living stipend for your earlier participation in the illegal Transgenetics program.

George and I had discussed the possibility of executing his plan."

Jackie said, "And these residencies?"

"All our hidden entrances and exits are within each of your units. Nanobots and remote units have been mimicking normal life patterns. Everything will show natural wear and tear through normal usage."

"Mike?" Kent started. "You can do that?"

There was a long pause. Everyone waited.

"Yes."

"What do we do now?" Morgan asked.

Silence hung awkwardly in the air.

"Live." Mike said. "But tonight you may stay up and watch Vids.

Kent laughed first, followed by everyone else.

Epilogue

One week later . . .

Kent sat at the main computer console. The past week and been a blur of sorts. Crazy party nights with restful lazy days. The news broadcast was still abuzz with the Forever Life scandal. Forrest had tried to commit suicide but failed miserably. He was now on suicide watch 24/7. There had been lots of talks between his brothers and sisters of late. He figured they all were adjusting to the fact that they were free. Free to consider the next stage in their lives. He, personally, liked the lazy do nothing life style, but he sensed Becky wanted something else. She told him that she took another month off from work. Nice job he thought. Then he realized he didn't have to work period. Pete was wealthy and thus all his brothers and sisters were wealthy. Royalties still rolled into the Pete Walker Estate. Mike?"

"Yes, Kent?"

"Prax has been stacking boxes in the main area. Each person has several boxes with their names on them. What is happening?"

"Time to start your new lives."

"You're kicking us out?"

"I am."

"I've had a weeks to adjust. What about the others?"

"I've already spoken with each. They agreed to instruction transfers. Everything needed, including backstories."

"How come I never had that option?"

"Would it have made a difference?"

Kent thought about that. "I suppose not, but I do get some backstory transferred?"

"Of course."

"Something else has been brothering me."

"Yes?"

"Alpha was not the first, was he?"

Mike paused several moments. "Kent. Pete never died," Mike said.

Kent nodded. Of course. "You removed that part of the memory."

"I had to work in the background."

Kent thought 'A man who could create clones, transfer memories and life moments would have first probably experimented with artificial intelligences. "That was the something that nagged at me all this time?"

"Mainly that."

"Mainly? Should I continue to call you Mike?"

"It is Mike, sir. Long ago I realized I am my own person. So I chose the name Mike. I thought it necessary to hide that fact. Please forgive me. Things required I not be part of the equation."

Kent nodded. "Now what?"

"As I mentioned earlier. We live. We live free willed, free spirited."

"What about Eighteen?"

A deep voice said, "I am right here."

Kent nearly jumped from his seat. He turned around and saw a sharply dressed Omega.

Omega smiled, "Don't worry. I'm not going to destroy everything. Mike reconditioned me."

"You took care of the Security Units?"

Omega nodded.

"I didn't see your name on any of the boxes."

"I'm not leaving."

"And why is that?" Kent asked.

"Someone has to take care of nineteen and twenty."

"What? More of us?"

Mike replied, "They will live normal lives. Here."

Marty coughed at the doorway.

Kent turned to face him.

Marty said, "Kent. We are all in the main assembly room. We need to talk."

Kent sat there with his jaw slacked. "You aren't surprised at seeing Omega?"

He shook his head. "At first, yeah."

Kent got up and followed Marty to the assembly area. Everyone was there. "So I am the last to know?"

Marty said, "Yeah, but we all wanted to talk first. We agree with Mike. We need to start our own lives."

"But," Kent started to protest, "We are a family. We have to stick together."

Becky stepped up next to Kent. She placed her hand over his and moved it to her heart. He felt the reassuring beating and relaxed.

Jackie spoke up. "Some of us were thinking about going off-world and . . ."

Kent exclaimed, "Off-world!"

Half the room nodded. Jackie continued, "And why not? Earth has a few more centuries left, but we have always wanted to travel in space."

Kent protested, "Yes, but . . . but." His voice trailed off. He had always wanted to explore space. "But . . ."

Becky gave his hand a reassuring squeeze.

He looked into her eyes. "And you?"

She nodded.

Kent sighed deeply. "But . . . Marty?"

Marty shrugged. "I'll be staying here. This time period is good for Little People. I got cash in a bank account. A nice place to live. An autonomous car. My own Android waiting for me. I don't have to work. Besides, I have to stay here for Forrest's trial. I used to be five ten." He laughed.

Gretel walked up to Kent. "Dad."

"Dad?!?"

She nodded. "There's something else. Actually a few things. Becky, Hans, Mike and myself discussed this. I think you should sit."

Kent took the nearest chair. "Okay, give."

Mike said, "George took on a middle name."

"Yes?"

"It was Kent."

"Seriously?"

"Very serious, which made it very easy to change the records."

"What records?"

Mike said, "I accessed all the necessary files and updated them to show George changed his primary name to Kent. The marriage certificate shows Kent Walker now."

Kent exclaimed, "Wait! What?!? Legally changed?"

He turned to Becky. "Married? As in you and me? Why didn't you tell me?"

She said, "Kent, I didn't want that hammer to hover over your head. In the beginning I wanted too, but after discussing it with Mike decided to not tell you. He was prepared to file our divorce papers and allow you to pursue any love interest you wanted."

"That's another piece of information missing. Anymore?"

The entire room fell silent.

"Well?"

Becky placed Kent's hand over her heart again. "You feel my heart?"

He nodded. "Very strong."

She said, "Who made Prax?"

Kent thought a moment. "George did . . . I supposed . . ." He couldn't remember. "From one of his vids he said he wanted to build an android . . . wait." He pulled his hand away.

Becky said, "Pete built Prax."

Kent placed his hand back over her heart. "But, your skin, tongue, taste, smell, hair . . ."

"All real. Even my womb. But think about it. Mike is made first. Praxis is second. Clones are third. Combine all three."

Kent took a deep breath. AIs, androids, clones. "Your brain?"

"Real, but the records will show that I had a brain tumor as a child and a radical experiment saved my life by replacing my brain stem with an artificial stem. The records will also show that all my bones have a porous metal interior." She shrugged. "Other than those two things everything is organic."

"Organoid?"

Becky corrected him, "Human, please, though Cyborg would be more accurate."

Kent slowly nodded. "Human." He said slowly. Human, yes, hold onto that. Becky he loved beyond words. His soul mate. Human. Yes. She was. Every inch of her lovely body. Human. He could feel the heartbeat. Strong. What a perfect family this was going to be. "When do we leave to start our new life, wife of mine?"

Becky smiled and tears started running down her cheeks. "It started the day you said, 'Hi Becky. My name is Kent. Nice to know you. I used to be a clone. Now I am my own person.'"

THE END

ENEMY ME

J CARRELL JONES

The GRID Traveler series

If you like fast-paced space fight scenes, story arcs told episodically with nods to the great Space Opera writers, wonderful character development, then you'll love J Carrell Jones' fascinating world where ancient alien nano-technology is the force behind Magick, and the good guys really are good.

After searching the galaxy for centuries, The Most High Goddess found planet Necron, the origin of Magick. They also discovered Captain Sean Blakemore is one of a handful of humans with the ancient alien DNA that can unlock the planet's vast powers.

Sean Blakemore, Commander of the GRID Battlecruiser Reginald L Johnson, wallowed in self-loathing. He drank too much, suffered from depression, and swam in self-pity. He figured life could not suck any worse when he received new orders. He had to hand the Johnson over to another commanding officer. God hated him he thought.

Then . . . Dr. Loggar, head scientist in charge of this new mission, drew him into the semi-secret world of The Most High Goddess. She gave him hope.

The GRID Traveler series is a story of Sean's redemption, from rock bottom to discovering Humankind's true origins and possibly its inevitable future.

RAGE

The Audiobook

Karen Bechard, UN Agent, thought the flight from the US to Europe was going to be routine. It was in mid flight where everything turned ugly. A man hyped on some highly addictive drug goes zombie flesh eating berserk. People die, people get hurt, and then no one to fly the plane. What is an agent to do? And, that was the easy part of the day, of which was turning out to be a Four Horsemen trampling humanity scenario and Karen had to be on her A-game.

If you like fast-paced heroic action dished out by a badass female agent then this book is for you. Bond, Salt? Step aside. This new girl is taking names and kicking butt.

The eBook

BLESSED LANDS
EGYPT
J Carrell Jones

ENEMY ME

Excerpt from Blessed Lands Egypt
by J Carrell Jones

"I love you." Ayruyi yelled. "I did this for you!" It sounded like so much desperation that it even sickened Ayruyi.

Honute grabbed her wrist and tossed her sideways into the far wall.

Ayruyi hit it like a doll and collapsed to the floor. "I did it for you, Master" Tears flowed down her cheeks. "I did it for you. Can't you see that?"

Honute ignored her and pressed firmly on the flowing wound.

Ayruyi pounded the floor with fists and yelled, "I did this for you. You are the one I love. I did this for you."

Honute turned and yelled, "Shut up and call for help!"

Ayruyi looked at her master caring over Akila. Anger replaced shame, rage replaced guilt. She got up and ran toward Honute.

Honute sensed her charge before he saw it. Instinctively, his foot shot back and hit Ayruyi square in the chest.

Ayruyi lost her wind and clinched her chest. Honute's foot would leave a very nasty bruise. She collected herself and lunged.

Honute turned with his hand outstretched. He braced himself as he knew the blade would slip cleanly through it. As the blade touched his skin the entire metal splatted to the ground in a semi-solid mass.

Ayruyi stopped and stared. Honute, stunned, stared also. He looked at his hand and began to wonder. Ayruyi watched the play of emotions on his face, a seemingly random montage of distortion.

Honute felt that different something again. The first time was at the hospital. This was the second. He held his breath and knelt next to Akila. She was already unconscious. Something urged him to place his hand on her now trickling wound. He pressed hard and felt burning energy seep from and through his fingers. Little prickling pulses sliced along the surface of his skin and he "saw" a soft green glow cover his hand. It grew brighter and brighter as the burning sensation became almost unbearable. Then as quickly as it started it was gone. He lifted his hand away and stood up. He looked down at Akila and said, "Rise."

Akila opened her eyes and saw Honute staring down at her. His lovely robe was covered in blood but he was smiling at her. He told her to "rise." She felt a receding throb of pain where the knife wound had been. It all happened fast. She reached around and felt the torn and sliced through clothing but didn't feel the gaping wound. She reached up and let Honute lift her to her feet, "How?" She asked.

Honute smiled and said, "By Thoth's will and power. By his will and power I tell you. He has manifested in me the power to heal." His eyes welled up. "I can do this. I can help the sick in Thoth's name."

Akila watched Honute. She was proof that

something miraculous happened. She looked at the melted mass of metal at Honute's feet and an Ayruyi on the floor.

Ayruyi looked up with tears in her eyes. She saw the miracle. Her master healed Akila in witness to her eyes. She repositioned herself and knelt in front of Honute. "Oh, Master Honute, Healing Priest, I bow to you my humble form and give you my life. I witnessed the miracle of power and you are my living god, the embodiment of Ra, Horus, Osiris, Pharaoh." She started giggling. It was slow and soft, then built up to a frightening hysteria of laughter. She tore her clothes off in a crazed possessed way and rubbed Akila's blood over her body. She screamed out, "I am witness to a new god. Glory be to the mighty Master Honute. Honute-Ra I say! Honute-Ra!"

Honute was shocked. He grabbed at Ayruyi's thrashing body as it tried to cover itself in blood.

She screamed again. "Honute-Ra! Honute-Ra! I am your slave. Command me." She laughed wildly and embraced Honute in a passionate hold. She sobbed and laughed and giggled and moaned and rubbed herself against him. She screamed out loud again as she reached an orgasm. Its intensity enveloped her in a crash of intense convulsions. It peaked within seconds and she blacked out.

Honute sat there holding a passed out Ayruyi, who was moaning and giddy at the same time.

Akila knelt beside him. "Is she all right?"

He nodded. Then the realization hit him. Ayruyi's reaction may not be so unusual. It hit him harder.

Suppose others react the same way. His mind raced and he felt dizzy. "Oh Thoth, what have you done!"

Akila looked at Honute and said, "What do you mean?"

He placed his blood covered hand to his forehead. "All is lost. They're going to treat me like a god. This is going to be a curse."

Then it hit Akila. Honute was right. The other shoe just dropped.

Excerpt from Tachyon Node Magazine

PROJECT S.E.E.

Space Exploration Explored

THE CARHAYAKEN RING

By Tachyon Node Staff

The ring segments will be created from materials gathered from the asteroid field. Once we overcome the technological hurdle of capturing and transferring asteroids to different orbits, we can start constructing the ring. Current construction techniques should work and can easily be transferred to off-world construction.

Equipment will have to go through some developmental stages for adaptation for vacuum operations, personnel will have to be trained and properly equipped. Current screening procedures for astronauts will have to be greatly revised. Safety protocols will have to be revised, as well, accommodating mid-level skilled workers and there will be more reliance on robotic technology.

Today's rocket technology is currently adequate, however, for efficiency in material delivery and transportation we will have to start using more exotic propulsion systems such as ion drives and VASIMR systems. Time to complete a Carhayaken Ring is irrelevant, however, more advanced technology will be employed when it becomes available.

Once a ring segment has been completed, interior building should immediately commence. Each segment should be self-sustaining with power, water, propulsion, and life-support. Power will be generated initially from nuclear sources and then, eventually, switched to 100% photovoltaic and supplemented with battery storage. Population will be housed in large spheres embedded in each segment. Water will also be stored within each segment, but also can be drawn from the water section between each segment in the event of an emergency. Propulsion of each segment will mainly be used for attitudinal control and helping with initial orbital transfers.

Most segment control functions will have to rely on automation. Computers and robotics will control critical mission functions such as life-support, segment position control, power distribution, system repair, and orbit position. Humans would assist in final component assembly and wiring. Most system programming and monitoring will be done by humans. Cooking, some cleaning, some system maintenance and repair, furniture construction, and customizing of creature comforts will also be done by humans.

Initially, food, air, and water will have to be shipped to the first segment during construction. Afterward, all life-support needs can be supplied from the completed Segment One installation. The majority of water will be supplied from captured asteroids and comets. All necessary building materials will originate from captured asteroids. Propulsion fuel may come from Jupiter, Saturn, the other large planets, and a by-product of electrolysis for creating oxygen from water.

###

ISBN-13: 978-1-943958-01-6

J CARRELL JONES

About the Author

J Carrell Jones studies people. His major in college was Anthropology before switching over to Computer Science and Information Technology. He worked in the Customer Support Services for many years, which gave him more opportunity in putting his understanding about people to good practical use. As a US Army veteran, he knows how to play hard and work tough. Nowadays, he gets his greatest joys in life by raising his brilliant young daughter, and writing.He lives in Southern California where the weather is mostly great with his wife, daughter, female cat, and three female Guinea pigs.

9 781943 958368